William Shakespeare's 1 Henry IV, aka Henry IV, Part 1: A Retelling in Prose

David Bruce

Published by David Bruce, 2022.

This is a work of fiction. Similarities to real people, places, or events are entirely coincidental.

WILLIAM SHAKESPEARE'S 1 HENRY IV, AKA HENRY IV, PART 1: A RETELLING IN PROSE

First edition. July 21, 2022.

Copyright © 2022 David Bruce.

ISBN: 979-8201800857

Written by David Bruce.

Table of Contents

Dedication

Dedicated to Carl Eugene Bruce and Josephine Saturday Bruce

My father, Carl Eugene Bruce, died on 24 October 2013. He used to work for Ohio Power, and at one time, his job was to shut off the electricity of people who had not paid their bills. He sometimes would find a home with an impoverished mother and some children. Instead of shutting off their electricity, he would tell the mother that she needed to pay her bill or soon her electricity would be shut off. He would write on a form that no one was home when he stopped by because if no one was home he did not have to shut off their electricity.

The best good deed that anyone ever did for my father occurred after a storm that knocked down many power lines. He and other linemen worked long hours and got wet and cold. Their feet were freezing because water got into their boots and soaked their socks. Fortunately, a kind woman gave my father and the other linemen dry socks to wear.

My mother, Josephine Saturday Bruce, died on 14 June 2003. She used to work at a store that sold clothing. One day, an impoverished mother with a baby clothed in rags walked into the store and started shoplifting in an interesting way: The mother took the rags off her baby and dressed the infant in new clothing. My mother knew that this mother could not afford to buy the clothing, but she helped the mother dress her baby and then she watched as the mother walked out of the store without paying.

My mother and my father both died at 7:40 p.m.

Cover Photograph for William Shakespeare's *1 Henry IV*, aka *Henry IV, Part 1*: A Retelling in Prose:

Public Domain

Falstaff am Tisch mit Weinkrug und Zinnbecher. Öl auf Leinwand, 39 x 31 cm, signiert und datiert 1910.

https://tinyurl.com/y45ksstm

Educate Yourself
Read Like A Wolf Eats
Be Excellent to Each Other
Books Then, Books Now, Books Forever

***

In this retelling, as in all my retellings, I have tried to make the work of literature accessible to modern readers who may lack some of the knowledge about mythology, religion, and history that the literary work's contemporary audience had.

Do you know a language other than English? If you do, I give you permission to translate this book, copyright your translation, publish or self-publish it, and keep all the royalties for yourself. (Do give me credit, of course, for the original retelling.)

I would like to see my retellings of classic literature used in schools, so I give permission to the country of Finland (and all other countries) to give copies of this book to all students forever. I also give permission to the state of Texas (and all other states) to give copies of this book to all students forever. I also give permission to all teachers to give copies of this book to all students forever.

Teachers need not actually teach my retellings. Teachers are welcome to give students copies of my books as background material. For example, if they are teaching Homer's *Iliad* and *Odyssey*, teachers are welcome to give students copies of my *Virgil's* Aeneid: *A Retelling in Prose* and tell students, "Here's another ancient epic you may want to read in your spare time."

CAST OF CHARACTERS

The Good Guys

King Henry the Fourth.

Henry, Prince of Wales, son to the King. Aka Prince Hal.

Prince John of Lancaster, son to the King.

Earl of Westmoreland.

Sir Walter Blunt.

The Rebels

Thomas Percy, Earl of Worcester.

Henry Percy, Earl of Northumberland.

Henry Percy, his son.

Edmund Mortimer, Earl of March.

Scroop, Archbishop of York.

Sir Michael, his Friend.

Archibald, Earl of Douglas.

Owen Glendower.

Sir Richard Vernon.

The Lowlifes

Sir John Falstaff.

Edward "Ned" Poins.

Gadshill.

Peto.

Bardolph.

The Women

Lady Percy, Wife to Hotspur.

Lady Mortimer, Daughter to Glendower.

Mrs. Quickly, Hostess in Eastcheap.

Other Characters

Lords, Officers, Sheriff, Vintner, Chamberlain, Drawers, Carriers, Travellers, and Attendants.

CHAPTER 1

— 1.1 —

In 1399, Henry Bolingbroke succeeded in deposing his first cousin King Richard II of England, thereby becoming King Henry IV. Even after becoming King, however, he ruled over an uneasy country, many citizens of which believed that he had unjustly seized the crown. After Richard II died, Henry IV vowed to go on a crusade to the Holy Land and return it to Christian hands. Political events, however, kept coming up that required delaying that crusade.

King Henry IV met with one of his younger sons, Lord John, who was Earl of Lancaster, as well as with the Earl of Westmoreland and Sir Walter Blunt, and others in his palace in London. King Henry IV was under great stress due to political and personal troubles.

Using the royal we, King Henry IV said, "We are shaken by events and wan with care, but let us find time and breath in this shaky and still-frightened peacetime to talk about the new battles that we intend to fight in distant foreign lands. No more will the English soil drink the blood of her children. No more will the English fields be filled with cutting war. No more will the English flowerets be bruised by the tread of armored warhorses. The soldiers of hostile forces that have recently opposed and killed each other in civil wars were all countrymen, as similar to each other as are shooting stars. Now, these formerly hostile forces shall all march as one in mutual well-ordered ranks. No more will they be opposed against acquaintances, relatives, and allies. They will be united for a common purpose. No more will the edge of war, as if it were an ill-sheathed knife, cut our people. Therefore, friends, we will hold a crusade and go as far as the sepulcher of Christ in Jerusalem. We are now the soldier of Christ, under Whose blessed cross we have been conscripted and for Whom we are pledged to fight. Therefore, we will raise an English army composed of people who were shaped in their mothers' wombs and born to chase away the pagans from those holy fields over whose acres walked those blessed feet which fourteen hundred years ago were nailed for our benefit to the bitter cross. For twelve months, we have been planning to do this. You know this, so we need not tell you our plans again."

He then ordered, "My noble kinsman Westmoreland, tell us what the council decided yesterday about planning this urgent crusade."

The Earl of Westmoreland replied, "My liege, we hotly discussed this crusade, and we had assigned many specific military responsibilities, but we were interrupted by a messenger bearing important news from Wales. The news was bad concerning the noble Edmund Mortimer, Earl of March. He led the men of Herefordshire to fight the lawless and wild Owen Glendower, who captured him. The Welshmen butchered a thousand men of Herefordshire. The Welshwomen did such a beastly shameless transformation to those corpses that it cannot be retold or spoken about except with much shame."

True, the Earl of Westmoreland thought. *The wild Welshwomen castrated the English corpses.*

King Henry IV said, "The news of this new battle must have necessarily stopped your debate about our crusade to the Holy Land."

Westmoreland replied, "This news and other news did that. Other news, even more disturbing and unwelcome, came from the north of England. On Holy-rood day, September 14, young Harry Percy — known also as the gallant Hotspur — fought the brave Earl of Douglas, that ever-valiant Scot, at the hill of Holmedon. The news we received was that they were fighting a serious and bloody battle with much firing of artillery. Our messenger left at the peak of the battle and so was unable to report who would win the battle."

"I have received more recent news than you about that battle," King Henry IV said. "A dear, truly devoted friend, Sir Walter Blunt, has newly alighted from his horse. He and his horse are stained with the various kinds of soil that lie between the hill of Holmedon and this palace of ours in London. He has brought us pleasant and welcome news: Hotspur has defeated the Earl of Douglas. Sir Walter Blunt himself saw the bloody corpses of ten thousand bold Scots and twenty-two knights heaped in piles on the plains by Holmedon. Hotspur has taken some nobles prisoner: Mordake, who is the Earl of Fife and the oldest son of the defeated Douglas; and the Earl of Athol, the Earl of Murray, the Earl of Angus, and the Earl of Menteith. Is not this an honorable spoil? Is not this a gallant prize? Ha, Westmoreland, is it not?"

"Truly," Westmoreland replied, "it is a conquest for a Prince to boast of."

"Indeed it is," King Henry IV said, "but you make me sad and make me sin in envy when you say that. I am envious that the Earl of Northumberland is the father to so blest a son as Hotspur. Anyone who wishes to speak of honor speaks about Hotspur. In a crowd of young men, Hotspur stands out; if he were a tree in a grove, he would be the very straightest tree in that grove. Hotspur is the darling and the pride of Fortune. I see people praise Hotspur, and then I look at my own oldest son, my young Harry — my Prince Hal and the future King of England — and I see debauchery and dishonor upon his brow. I wish that I could prove that a mischievous fairy had come by when the two Harrys were infants and had swapped them! In that case, Hotspur would be my son, and Prince Hal would be the son of the Earl of Northumberland. Such thinking is sinful. But let us move on to other matters. What is your opinion of young Hotspur's pride? He has sent word to me that he shall deliver to me, from all his prisoners, only one: Mordake, the Earl of Fife. He has sent word to me that he will keep all the other prisoners. Hotspur knows that he cannot keep as prisoner Mordake, who is of royal blood, but all prisoners are required to be turned over to me, the King, so that we can ransom them."

Westmoreland replied, "Hotspur must be following the advice of Thomas Percy, the Earl of Worcester, who is his uncle. Worcester is opposed to you in every way possible, and his advice is making Hotspur proud and resistant to your authority. He is like a proud bird that preens its feathers and raises its crest."

"I have sent word to Hotspur to come to me and to answer for his actions," King Henry IV said. "Because of this, I must for a while put aside my crusade to Jerusalem. On Wednesday, we will meet with the council at Windsor. Inform all the lords about the meeting, and then quickly return here. More is to be said and to be done. I am angry now, and I do not wish to speak publicly."

"I will do as you wish, my liege," Westmoreland said.

Prince Hal, who was a young man, and Sir John Falstaff, who was an old, obese knight who lived by committing crimes and entertaining people with his wit, were talking together in a place in London where the Prince sometimes stayed.

Falstaff asked, "Hal, what time of day is it, lad?"

Hal replied, "You are so fat-witted because of your drinking of that Spanish white wine we call sack and because of your unbuttoning your pants after supper and sleeping upon benches until afternoon that you have forgotten to ask whatever it is that you truly want to know. What the Devil do you have to do with the time of the day? Unless hours were cups of sack and minutes were castrated cocks fattened for eating — capons — and clocks were the tongues of women who run brothels and dials were the signs of whorehouses and the blessed Sun himself were a beautiful hot prostitute wearing a flame-colored dress made of taffeta, I see no reason why you need to ask the time of the day."

"You make a good point, Hal," Falstaff said. "Those of us who live by robbing travelers and taking their wallets live by the time of the Moon and the seven stars, and not by the time of Phoebus Apollo, that wandering knight so fair who drives the chariot of the Sun across the sky each day. Dear rogue, please, when you are King, God save your grace — oops, I should say 'God save your majesty' because you have no grace."

"What, none?" Prince Hal asked. "I have no sense of propriety, no sense of virtue?"

"No, you don't, Prince Hal," Falstaff said, "In fact, you don't have enough grace to say a prayer before eating an egg and butter."

"Get to the point," Prince Hal said. "When I am King, what?"

"I have a request," Falstaff said. "When you are King, don't allow those of us who are squires of the night to be called thieves of the day. True, we stay up at night and sleep during the day — we commit our robberies at night. But let us be called by dignified names. Let us be called Diana the Moon goddess' foresters. Let us be called gentlemen of the shade. Let us be called servants of the Moon. And let men say that we are men of good government or conduct because we are governed, as the sea and its tides are, by our noble and chaste mistress the Moon, under whose countenance we steal."

"You speak truly," Prince Hal said. "Your comparison is apt. The fortune of us who are the Moon's men ebbs and flows like the sea and its tides, because we are governed, as the sea and its tides are, by the Moon. This I can prove with an example. A wallet filled with gold that was resolutely robbed from a traveler on Monday night is dissolutely spent on Tuesday morning. The money is gotten by crying, 'Put your hands up!' And it is spent by crying, 'Sack! Bring in more sack!' We see the ebb when the robber stands at the foot of a ladder leading to a gallows, and we see the flow or flood when the robber is standing at the top of the gallows with a rope around his neck."

"By the Lord, you speak the truth, lad," Falstaff said. Uncomfortable at the thought of hanging, a very real possibility in his life, he changed the subject: "Don't you think that the Hostess of the tavern is a most sweet wench?"

"She is as sweet as the honey from the hills around Syracuse in Sicily, my old lad of the Castle," Prince Hal replied. "Of course, you should know. After all, you know well the London brothel that roisterers everywhere call the Castle. And the Castle is a place where the Hostess of the tavern could very well work. By the way, don't you think that a buff jerkin is a most sweet robe of durance?"

"The Sheriff's officers wear buff jerkins because they are made of leather and so wear well and endure, but of course you mean durance in the sense of imprisonment," Falstaff complained. "You keep bringing up things that could form part of my future life. Why are you making these particular quips and jests? Why should I want to hear about buff jerkins? I would prefer to hear about the plague!"

"Why should I want to hear about the Hostess of the tavern?" Prince Hal replied. "I would prefer to hear about the pox!"

"The pox is syphilis," Falstaff said. "If you have much to do with the Hostess of the tavern, you are very likely to hear about syphilis. Remember, Hal, you have called her to a reckoning many times."

"The reckonings I have called her to have been to pay our bills for food and drink," Prince Hal said. "I have never needed to pay reckonings for her other business — the one involving women and bedrooms. Have I ever asked you to pay even part of a bill?"

"No, Prince Hal," Falstaff said. "I'll give you your due. You have always paid the entire bill."

"Yes, I have, both here and elsewhere, as long as my money held out," Prince Hal said. "And when I have run out of money, I have used my credit."

"Yes, you have," Falstaff said. "And you have used so much credit that it is fortunate that it is here apparent that you are heir apparent. But, Hal, let ask you whether there will be gallows standing in England when you are King? Will courageous highwaymen continue to be collared by the overly long arm of the law? Please, Hal, when you are King, do not hang thieves."

"I won't, but you will," Prince Hal said.

"Shall I hang thieves?" Falstaff said. "Oh, joy! By the Lord, I'll be an excellent judge."

"You are already judging incorrectly," Prince Hal said. "I mean that you will do the hanging and therefore become an excellent hangman."

"If you say so, Hal," Falstaff said. "Hanging thieves is much better than hanging around in the court."

"Would you hang out to obtain suits?" Prince Hal asked.

"If I hung out in court, I would obtain lawsuits, but if I were a hangman, I would obtain suits of clothing because the clothing of the hung is forfeited to the hangman. Truly, the hangman does not have a lean wardrobe. But all this talk of hanging is making me as melancholy as a tomcat howling at night or a bear tormented by dogs."

"Or an old, toothless lion, or a sad note on a lover's lute."

"Yes, or the drone of a single note played on a Lincolnshire bagpipe."

"What about a timorous rabbit, or the melancholy of Moorditch?"

"Moorditch, ugh!" Falstaff said. "That foul drainage ditch! That sewer where lepers and insane people beg! Hal, you make the most unsavory comparisons. Why am I surprised! You are prone to making similes, you rascally, sweet young Prince."

Falstaff decided to imitate a Puritan, as he so often did, and said, "But, Hal, please, trouble me no more with worldly considerations. I wish to God that you and I knew where a supply of good reputations could be bought. An old lord of the council criticized me the other day in the street because I allow you to be my friend, but I ignored him even though he made some good points. Yes, indeed, he talked very wisely, and in the street, too."

"You did well because wisdom cries out in the streets, and no man regards it," Prince Hal said, thinking that if Falstaff were going to pretend to be a holy man that he would respond by paraphrasing Proverbs 1:20.

"You have a talent for twisting scripture to serve your ends," Falstaff said, "and you have a talent for corrupting people — even saints! You have done much harm to me by corrupting me, Hal. I pray that God forgives you for it! Before I knew you, Hal, I knew nothing of evil. But now that I know you, Hal, I am, if a man should speak truly, little better than one of the wicked. I must repent my life, and I will reform and give my life to the Lord. If I do not, I am a villain and I will be damned to Hell. But I have no intention of being damned — not even for the son of a King."

"Where shall we steal a wallet tomorrow, Jack?" Prince Hal asked Falstaff.

"By God, wherever you want," Falstaff said enthusiastically. "I will make up one of the members in your band of robbers. If I do not, call me a villain and disgrace me."

"I can see that you want to reform your life," Prince Hal said. "A moment ago you were praying to God, and now you are ready to be a thief."

Falstaff joked, "Why, Hal, being a thief is my vocation, Hal. It is no sin for a man to labor in his vocation."

A thief named Edward Poins entered the room. He was on terms of great familiarity with Falstaff and Prince Hal.

Falstaff said, "Welcome, Poins! Now we will learn whether our friend Gadshill has set up a robbery for us to perform. If men were able to be saved by merit, what hole in hell would be hot enough for Gadshill and his evil deeds? He is the most unparalleled villain who ever cried 'Put your hands up!' to a honest man."

True, Prince Hal thought, *Gadshill takes his name — the only one I know — from Gad's Hill, the scene of many, many robberies.*

"Good day, Ed," Prince Hal said to Ned Poins.

"Good day, sweet Hal," Poins replied.

To Falstaff, Poins said, "How are you, Monsieur Remorse? Are you still repenting your sins — or pretending to? How are you, Sir John Sack and Sugar? Are you still engaging in your favorite hobbies — drinking too much and increasing the size of your belly? Jack, are you and the Devil still tussling over your soul, which you sold to him for a cup of Madeira wine and a cold chicken leg on Good Friday, the most holy of fast days?"

"Sir John will keep his word and his agreement," Prince Hal said. "The Devil shall get Falstaff's soul, for Falstaff will not break the proverb that says to give the Devil his due."

Poins said to Falstaff, "In that case, you are damned because you are keeping your word to the Devil. How odd to be damned for keeping one's word."

"Falstaff would have been damned in any case," Prince Hal said. "If he did not keep his word to the Devil, he would be damned for not keeping his word."

Poins said, "Now to business. Be at Gad's Hill by 4 a.m. Pilgrims are going to the holy shrine at Canterbury to make rich donations, and traders are riding to London with fat wallets. I have masks for all of you, and each of you has his own horse. Gadshill will be spending the night in an inn in Rochester. I have already ordered supper for tomorrow night at our favorite tavern in Eastcheap. We could do this robbery in our sleep. If you will go with me and be robbers, I will stuff your wallets full of money; if you will not, stay at home and be hanged."

"Ed," Falstaff said, "if I stay at home and do not go with you, I'll turn state's evidence and have you hanged for going."

"You're joking, chipmunk cheeks," Poins said. "You need the money from the robbery. I have never known you when you did not need money from a robbery."

"Hal, will you make up one of our band of robbers?" Falstaff asked.

"Who? I?" Prince Hal asked, shocked. "Am I a thief? No, I am not. I will not go with you."

Prince Hal thought, *Falstaff would like for me to be a thief. He truly is a false staff. He would like for me to be an alcoholic and a criminal. That way, he could control me, and later, after I am King, he could loot all of England. Still, he can be great fun to be around.*

"Hal," Falstaff said, "no honesty, manhood, or good fellowship are in you and it is false that you come from the blood royal, if you lack the courage to rob a man for ten shillings, which as you know, is the monetary worth of our English coin the royal."

Prince Hal replied, "I will be a madcap and act on wild impulses."

"That's well said," Falstaff said.

"I lied," Prince Hal said. "I will stay at home."

"By the Lord, then I'll be a traitor," Falstaff said, "when you are King."

"So be it," Prince Hal said. "I don't care."

Poins said, "Sir John, please leave the Prince and me alone. I will give him reasons why he should join our band of robbers early tomorrow morning. I will persuade him to go with us."

Falstaff said to Poins, "May God give you the spirit of persuasion and may Hal profit from what you tell him, so that what you speak may move Hal and what he hears he shall believe. That way, the true Prince may, for the sake of entertainment, prove a false thief. We poor criminals need royal protection. Farewell. If you need me, I will be at my favorite tavern in Eastcheap."

"Farewell, old man with the vigor of a young robber," Prince Hal said. "If you were a summer, you would last until November 1: All-Saints Day."

Falstaff departed, and Poins said to Prince Hal, "Please, my good sweet honey lord, ride with us tomorrow. I have a practical joke that I want to execute that I cannot manage alone. Falstaff, Bardolph, Peto, and Gadshill shall rob those men that I have already told you about. You and I will not be with them. When they have robbed the travelers and taken their money, you and I will rob the robbers. If we do not, then cut my head from off my shoulders."

Prince Hal was intrigued, but he was cautious. He said, "You and I will have to separate ourselves from the four robbers. How can we do that?"

Poins replied, "You and I will set forth before or after them, and we will appoint a place to meet before the robbery, but we will not show up there. Falstaff, Bardolph, Peto, and Gadshill will then commit the robbery by themselves. As soon as they have the money, you and I shall set upon them and rob them."

Still cautious, Prince Hal said, "It is very likely that they will recognize us because of our horses and our clothing, and simply because they know us so well."

"I have thought of that," Poins said. "They will not see our horses. I'll tie them in the wood. They will know the masks that I have brought, but we will change masks. Also, I have some garments made of buckram cloth that we can wear over our clothing."

"One more thing," Prince Hal said. "It will be the two of us trying to rob the four of them. The odds are not in our favor."

Poins replied, "I know that two of them are cowards who will readily turn their backs to us and run away, and if a third fights longer than he sees reason to, I vow never to fight again. Listen: The point of this practical joke is to hear the outrageous lies that fat Falstaff will tell when we meet to eat our supper. He will swear that he fought at least thirty swordsmen. He will describe the parries he made and the blows he took and the dangers he faced. Then you and I will tell him what really happened, and we will laugh at him."

Prince Hal thought that the reward outweighed the risk, and so he said, "Let's do it. Get everything we need, and we will play this practical joke. Tomorrow night, we will meet with the would-be robbers in Eastcheap. There we will listen to Falstaff tell his lies. Farewell."

"Farewell, my lord," Poins said, then departed.

Now alone, Prince Hal said to himself, "I know all of you for the robbers and lowlifes you are, and for a while I will allow you to commit your crimes and follow your idle, undisciplined inclinations. In so doing, I will imitate the Sun, which allows ugly storm clouds to cover up his beauty and hide him from the world. When the Sun decides to reveal again his glorious self, he will be marveled at all the more because of his absence and because he broke through the ugly storm clouds that seemed to be about to strangle him. If every day of the year were holidays during which men sought entertainments, to seek entertainments would be as tedious as going to work. But when holidays seldom come, they are desired. Good things that are rare are the most pleasing. Someday, I will stop my riotous and unworthy behavior, and I will accept the responsibilities of being a Crown Prince — responsibilities that I never sought but that came to me because of who my father is. I will make it known that I am so much better than I act now. Men will expect the worst from me, but I will give them my best. I will be like bright metal lying on dark soil. My riotous past will set off my goodness to a greater extent than goodness alone without a riotous past could ever appear. I will live a riotous life now, but I have a plan. I will reform when men think it is most unlikely that I will reform."

In the council chamber of Windsor Castle, King Henry IV met with the nobles from the North who had lately been giving him trouble: Hotspur; Hotspur's father, the Earl of Northumberland; and Hotspur's uncle, the Earl of Worcester. Also present were the King's good and loyal friend Sir Walter Blunt and other people. King Henry IV was angry at Hotspur because Hotspur had not sent him the prisoners that he had captured at the Battle of Holmedon on 14 September 1402.

King Henry IV said, "My blood has been too cold and temperate to be quickly angered by your insults to me. Because you have found me to be so lenient and so mild, you have tried my patience. Know that I will from now on be what my position requires me to be, a King who is mighty and to be feared, rather than the temperate and mild person I am by nature. I have been as smooth as oil and as soft as young down plucked from birds, and therefore you have not been giving me the respect that the proud pay only to the powerful."

Worcester replied, "Our house, my sovereign liege, does not deserve to be so criticized by you. You are using the scourge of greatness on us, but it is our family — the Percys — who helped to make you King of England. We supported you when you deposed King Richard II."

Northumberland started to speak, "My lord — "

But King Henry IV knew how to divide and conquer. He interrupted Northumberland and ordered, "Worcester, leave this room immediately. I see defiance and disobedience in your eyes. Your attitude is too bold and imperious. A King does not permit any of his subjects to angrily frown in his presence. You have my permission — and my order — to leave. If we need you or your counsel, we will send for you."

Although angry, Worcester bowed and left the room.

King Henry IV said to Northumberland, "You were about to speak."

"Yes, my good lord," Northumberland said. "Those prisoners that were demanded in your highness' name after Hotspur had captured them at Holmedon were not, he says, denied with such vehemence as was reported to your majesty. The report erred either because of malice or because of a misunderstanding. My son, Hotspur, is not guilty of what he has been accused."

Hotspur said, "My King, I did deny you no prisoners. But I remember, after the battle was over, when I was drained after the excitement of battle and extreme toil, when I was breathless and faint, leaning upon my sword, a certain lord came to me. He was neat, clean, and fashionably dressed, as fresh as a bridegroom, and his chin was recently fashionably clipped in a manner not designating a soldier — his chin looked like the stubble left on a field after the harvest. He wore perfume and smelled like a person who makes women's hats. Between his finger and his thumb, he held a perfume-box, which every so often he held up to his nose and sniffed and then sneezed. He smiled and he talked, but when the soldiers carried dead bodies near him, he became angry and called them uneducated and rude lowlifes because they had brought a foul, disgusting corpse between the wind and himself, thus forcing him to smell it. With many fancy and effeminate words, he questioned me. Among other things, he demanded my prisoners on your Majesty's behalf. I was in pain because my wounds were cold, and I was irritated because I was pestered with this perfumed parrot. Out of my pain and my impatience, I answered ... negligently ... I know not what. I said that he should take the prisoners, or I said that he should not take the prisoners. I don't remember because he made me so mad because he gleamed due to being so clean — and because he smelled so sweet and talked just like a waiting-gentlewoman when he spoke of guns and drums and wounds. Can you believe it? He told me that the best thing on Earth was spermaceti — which he said comes from whales — for an inward bruise. He also said that it was a great pity that villainous salt-petre should be dug out of the bowels of the harmless Earth and used for gunpowder to cowardly destroy so many good brave men. He also said that if it weren't for these vile guns, he himself would have been a soldier. This silly, incoherent chatter of his, my lord, I answered absent-mindedly, as I said, and I beg you not to let his report cause trouble between me and your Majesty, whom I hold in high respect."

Sir Walter Blunt, a good friend and advisor to King Henry IV, said to the King, "Considering the circumstances, my good lord, whatever Hotspur said to such a person at such a time and in such a place may reasonably be allowed to die and not discredit Hotspur now or later, provided that he make all things right with you now."

"But he is not making all things right!" King Henry IV said. "Even now, he will not give me his prisoners except with conditions. He demands that we at our own expense immediately ransom his brother-in-law, the foolish Mortimer, who, I believe, betrayed his men to that great magician, damned Glendower, and got one thousand of them killed by the magician whom he was supposed to fight. We also have learned that Mortimer has recently married Glendower's daughter. Shall our treasury be emptied so that Mortimer can return home again? Shall we aid a traitor? Shall we bargain with the enemy for the return of a traitor? Should I ransom a poor and defeated general who cowardly surrendered? Let him starve in the barren mountains! No one who asks me for even one penny to ransom the traitor Mortimer and bring him home shall ever be my friend."

"Mortimer a traitor!" Hotspur exclaimed. "He never faltered, my King, except through the fortunes of war. The proof lies in all those wounds — open like mouths — that he received while courageously fighting on the grassy bank of the Severn River. All alone, man against man, Mortimer battled great Glendower for close to an hour. Three times they stopped to catch their breath and three times, by mutual agreement, they drank from the swiftly flowing river. Their blood dripped into the water, which it discolored. As if frightened by its bloody water, the river carried it away and hid it in the reeds by its bank. Never has base and rotten traitorship disguised its treachery with such deadly wounds. Never could the noble Mortimer receive so many wounds, all of them willingly, if he were a traitor. Therefore, let him not be slandered by the title of traitor."

"You are not telling the truth about Mortimer," King Henry IV said. "Those are lies. Mortimer never fought Glendower — he would just as soon fight the Devil in single combat as he would Glendower. Aren't you ashamed to be telling such lies? Boy, from now on let me not hear you talk about Mortimer. And send me your prisoners by the speediest means possible — or else. Lord Northumberland, we order you to return to your Northern home with your son. Hotspur, and send us your prisoners, or you will regret it."

King Henry IV departed along with Sir Walter Blunt and others.

Hotspur was angry: "If the Devil himself should come and roar for my prisoners, I will not send them to the King. In fact, I will go to the King right now and tell him so. I will feel better after I tell the King what I really think, even if I lose my head by so doing."

His father, the Earl of Northumberland, said, "Are you drunk with anger? Stay here. Wait awhile. Look, here comes your uncle, the Earl of Worcester."

Worcester entered the room.

Hotspur was still angry and said, "The King orders me not to speak of Mortimer? I will speak of him, and let my soul lack mercy and not make it to Heaven if I do not join forces with Mortimer and fight on his side. In fighting for Mortimer, I will be willing to empty all my veins and shed my dear blood drop by drop in the dust, but by fighting for Mortimer I will raise the downtrod Mortimer as high in the air as this ungrateful and malignant Henry Bolingbroke, whom people call King Henry IV."

Northumberland said to Worcester, "Brother, the King has made your nephew mad."

"What caused this anger after I left?" Worcester asked.

Hotspur replied, "Bolingbroke said that he will indeed have all my prisoners, and when I urged again that he ransom Mortimer, my wife's brother, then his cheek looked pale, and on my face he turned a fearful look, trembling even at the name of Mortimer."

Worcester replied, "I cannot blame him for being afraid of the name of Mortimer. Didn't the late King Richard II proclaim that Mortimer was the heir to the throne?"

"He did," Northumberland said. "I myself heard the proclamation. Afterward, King Richard II — may God pardon us for our wrongs committed against him when we helped Bolingbroke to overthrow him! — set forth on his Irish expedition, which Richard cut short to return to England, where he was deposed and then murdered."

"Because of the murder of King Richard II, we Percys are foully spoken of and defamed by the world's wide mouth. The citizens of England are scandalized by our behavior in helping Bolingbroke and deposing Richard. We are even blamed for the murder of Richard."

"This news about Mortimer is new to me," Hotspur said. "Did King Richard II really proclaim Mortimer, my brother-in-law, to be next in line to the throne?"

Northumberland replied, "He did; I myself did hear it."

Hotspur said, "Then I cannot blame King Henry IV for wanting Mortimer to starve in the barren mountains. But is it right that you who set the crown on the head of Bolingbroke, who forgets the service that you have done for him and for whose sake you have suffered a loss of reputation, should have to suffer a world of curses when you were only the accomplices and means? When a man is hanged, who should be blamed for that man's death? The rope? The ladder? Or the hangman? Forgive me for using that comparison to show the perilous situation you are in under this cunning King and the low rank that he assigns to you. Are you willing to have bad things spoken about you now at this time and to have bad things written about you in history books that have yet to be written? Do you want to go down in history as noble and powerful men who did such an unjust deed as both of you — may God forgive you! — have done? You deposed King Richard II, that sweet lovely rose, and then you put on the throne this canker-rose — this ulcer — named Bolingbroke. And are you willing to be shamed by its being recorded that this man for whom you have done so much and for whom you have lost your good reputation should, having fooled you, now discard you? No. Time still remains for you to redeem your reputations and show yourselves to be good people. Get revenge for the jeering and disdain and contempt thrown at you by this proud King, who studies day and night to repay all the debt he owes to you — by killing you! Therefore, I say —"

Worcester interrupted Hotspur, "Be quiet, nephew. Say no more. Allow me to now metaphorically open a secret book so that I can read to your righteous anger and sense of grievance matter deep and dangerous, as full of peril and adventure as is a man who unsteadily walks over a loudly roaring current while using a spear as a bridge. Because of your anger, I am sure that you will be quick to understand me."

Because Hotspur, who was able to tell that his uncle was going to talk of rebelling against the King, was caught up in his hope of gaining glory on a battlefield, he expressed his opinions out loud instead of allowing his father and uncle to talk.

"If the man falls into the river," Hotspur said, "then it is a loss — and possibly a death — for him, whether he sinks immediately or swims. Let danger and honor meet and fight in the center of a battlefield. The blood moves more quickly when hunting a lion than when hunting a hare."

Northumberland said, "Imagination of some great exploit is making Hotspur lose his self-control."

Hotspur added, mostly to himself, "By Heaven, I think it would be an easy leap to jump up and pluck bright honor from the pale-faced Moon or to dive to the bottom of the sea, where a fathom-line could never reach the bottom, and pluck up drowned honor by her wet locks of hair. Let the person who rescues honor wear — without a rival — all her favors. Let the hero have *all* the honors — let there be no pathetic sharing of honors!"

"Hotspur is lost in his imagination," Worcester said to Northumberland. "He is not paying attention to the people who need his attention: you and I, who are in front of him."

Worcester then said, "Hotspur, please give me your attention."

"Pardon me," Hotspur said.

"These noble Scots who are your prisoners —"

Hotspur interrupted, "I'll keep them all! By God, he shall not have a Scot of them! No, if a Scot would save his soul, he shall not get one from me! I swear that I'll keep them!"

"You are off and running on your own tangent again and paying no attention to me," Worcester said. "As I said, you shall keep your prisoners."

"I certainly will," Hotspur said. "That's settled. King Henry IV said that he would not ransom Mortimer. He forbade me to mention Mortimer, but I will go to the King when he is asleep and in his ear I will shout 'Mortimer!' I know — I will get a starling and have it taught to speak nothing but the name 'Mortimer' and I will give it to the King so that he will be angry whenever the starling speaks!"

"Hotspur, listen to me for a moment," Worcester said.

Hotspur ignored Worchester and continued his rant: "From this moment I will think about nothing except how to gall and annoy this Bolingbroke and his son the lowlife Prince of Wales. I would kill Prince Hal with a pot of poisoned ale except that I think his father does not love him and would prefer that he meet with an accident or 'accident' that would take away his life. And why wouldn't he, given the company that Prince Hal keeps?"

"Farewell, Hotspur," Worcester said. "I will talk to you when you are ready to listen to me."

Northumberland said to Hotspur, "You are acting as if you were stung by wasps. You are an impatient fool who is behaving like a woman who talks continuously and never stops to listen."

Hotspur replied, "I am angry. It is as if I were whipped and beaten with sticks, stung by nettles, and stung by ants whenever I hear of this vile politician — this deceitful schemer — Bolingbroke. When King Richard II was still alive — what is that place called? Damn! I can't remember! It is in Gloustershire. There I first bowed my knee to this King of Smiles, this Bolingbroke when, my father, you and he came back from Ravenspurgh. You, my father, had gone to take sides with Bolingbroke and fight for him against King Richard II. Richard's uncle the madcap Duke of York dwelled there."

"You mean Berkeley castle," Northumberland said.

"Yes, that's it," Hotspur said. "What sugary flattery that fawning greyhound fed to me! He said, 'The promise of his childhood has come to fruition.' He called me 'gentle Harry Percy' and 'kind cousin.' May the Devil take such flatterers! Well, forgive me for ranting. Good uncle, tell your tale; I have finished."

"If you have not yet finished, start raving again," Worcester said sarcastically to him. "We will wait until you are done."

"I am done. I swear it," Hotspur said.

"Once more, let us talk about your Scottish prisoners," Worcester said. "Release your prisoners immediately without requiring a ransom. Mordake, the son of the Earl of Douglas, is one of your prisoners. Use that fact to raise an army of troops from Scotland. You will be given that army for several reasons that I shall write down in a letter and send to you."

Worcester said to Northumberland, "While Hotspur, your son, is busily employed in Scotland, you will make an ally of the Archbishop, that well-beloved noble prelate."

"You mean the Archbishop of York, don't you?" Northumberland asked.

"Yes," Worcester said. "He begrudges the death of his brother, the Lord Scroop, whom King Henry IV ordered to be executed at Bristol. The Archbishop has thought about rebellion, plotted rebellion, and decided definitely to rebel against the King. He is waiting for the right time to rebel. I say this not as a guess, but as what I know to be fact."

"I understand what is going on," Hotspur said. "It is a good plan. It will succeed."

"Don't be too hasty," Northumberland said. "The plot has not yet been set in motion. You don't want to let your dogs loose until the hunt begins."

"This plan is a noble plan that shall succeed," Hotspur said. "An army from Scotland and an army from York in the North of England will join with Mortimer, who will lead an army from Wales, right?"

Worcester replied, "Yes."

"This rebellion is well planned," Hotspur said.

Worcester said, "We have good reason to set this revolt quickly in motion. We can save our heads only by raising armies. No matter how carefully we act and try to please the King, he will always think that he is in our debt because we helped him to become King. He will also continue to think that we are unhappy because he has not sufficiently rewarded us. Therefore, the King will find a way to solve his problem — by killing us. He has already made us a stranger to any signs of his approval."

"Yes, he has done that," Hotspur said. "We'll be revenged on him."

"Hotspur, farewell," Worcester said. "Don't do anything except what I tell you to do in the letters to you that I shall send. When the time is ripe, which it soon will be, I will secretly go to Glendower and Lord Mortimer. You and the Scot Douglas and our united armies will meet together, and we will bear our fortunes on our own strong arms — our fortunes that are at the present time so uncertain."

Northumberland said to Worcester, "Farewell, good brother. We shall thrive, I trust."

Hotspur said to Worcester, "Farewell, uncle. Let the hours be short until battlefields and the blows and groans of battle applaud our cause!"

CHAPTER 2

— 2.1 —

A carrier — a transporter of goods — carrying a lantern entered the yard of an inn on the London-Canterbury Road and said, "Heigh-ho! If it isn't four in the morning, I'll be hanged. The Big Dipper is over the new chimney and still our horses have not been made ready. Groom!"

From inside the inn, the groom in charge of the horses said, "Coming! Coming!"

The first carrier said to a second carrier who was walking toward him, "Please, Tom, give the saddle of Cut, my horse, a few whacks to make it soft, and put some tufts of wool underneath the pommel of the saddle so that the padding makes the horse more comfortable. The poor nag is chafed by the saddle in between the shoulders."

Tom, the second carrier, said, "The peas and beans used in the horse feed at this inn are as damp as a dog, and that is a quick way to give the poor nags worms. This stable has gone to Hell since Robin Ostler died."

The first carrier replied, "Poor fellow, he was never happy since the price of oats rose; it was the death of him."

Tom said, "I think this is the worst inn in all London road when it comes to fleas: I have been bitten so much that my red spots make me look like the red-spotted fish known as a tench."

"That's a good comparison," the first carrier said. "By God, even though the Christian Kings get the most of everything, no King could surpass the number of flea bites I have received since midnight."

Tom said, "This inn won't even give us a chamber pot, and so we pee in the fireplace, and the urine helps the fleas to breed like rabbits."

The first carrier called, "Groom! Come here! Hurry up, damn it!"

They began to talk about their deliveries.

Tom said, "I have a ham and two roots of ginger that I need to deliver in Charing Cross."

The first carrier said, "The turkeys in my basket are quite starved — they are thin!"

He yelled for the groom, "Come here! Damn you! Can't you see me? Can't you hear me? Taking a drink is good, and so is hitting you on the head. Call me a villain if that is not true. Come here! You have a job to do!"

Gadshill, the highwayman who collected information about people whom he and his friends could rob, walked into the yard of the inn.

"Good morning, carriers," he said. "What time is it?"

The first carrier was suspicious for good reason: The inn was located in an area noted for robberies. Although he knew that the time was after 4 a.m., he did not want to give this stranger any information that could help him to commit a robbery, especially of the two carriers and their fellow travelers. He worried that this stranger might want information about when they would leave the inn and about where they were traveling.

The first carrier told Gadshill, "I think it is two o'clock."

"Please lend me your lantern so that I can see my gelding in the stable," Gadshill said to the first carrier.

The first carrier, afraid that Gadshill would steal the lantern, replied, "No, by God! My mother did not raise me to be a fool."

Gadshill then said to Tom, the second carrier, "Please lend me your lantern."

Tom replied, "When would I lend you my lantern? When it's a cold day in Hell, that's when — or the day after you are hanged!"

Gadshill asked, "What time do you think that you will arrive in London?"

Tom kept his answer vague: "Time enough to go to bed with a candle, I promise you."

Tom said to the first carrier, "Come, neighbor Mugs, let's talk to the gentlemen. They will accompany us."

Quietly, so that Gadshill would not hear him, Tom added, "They want to travel in a group because they have a valuable load."

The two carriers departed, and Gadshill called a confederate in the inn to come out and talk to him: "Chamberlain!"

The chamberlain attended to the bedrooms in the inn and therefore was able to overhear conversations and to learn much about the occupants at the inn.

The chamberlain arrived and said, "As a pickpocket would say, 'I am so close to you that I could put my hand in your pockets.'"

Gadshill replied, "That is as apt as saying, 'As a chamberlain would say, "I am so close to you that I could put my hand in your pockets."' You are very much like a pickpocket except the pickpocket does the actual stealing while you gather the information that leads to the theft."

"Good morning, Mr. Gadshill," the chamberlain said. "What I told you last night still holds true. A rich farmer from Kent has with him three hundred marks — a unit of money — in gold. I heard him tell it to one of his companions last night at supper: a kind of revenue officer — someone who is also carrying an abundance of valuables, although I do not know specifically what. They are already awake and have ordered eggs and butter for their breakfast. They will depart soon."

"They have a date to keep with Saint Nicholas' clerks, aka highwaymen," Gadshill said. "Traveling thieves are fortunate that Saint Nicholas is the patron saint of travelers, which I presume includes highwaymen. If these two people don't keep their date with robbers, I will give you my neck."

"I don't want your neck," the chamberlain said. "Please keep it for the hangman. I know that you worship Saint Nicholas as truly as a false man can."

"You need not talk to me about a hangman," Gadshill said. "If I hang, I will be part of a fat pair on the gallows because Sir John will hang with me, and you know that he is not starving. But I will work tonight with other highwaymen you do not know and cannot even dream of, people high in society who will rob for the sport of it, who will give robbers some class, and who, if we run into trouble, will — if only to help themselves — make everything for us all right. I will be accompanied by no footloose vagabonds, no people with long staffs who would pull a man from off his horse to steal sixpence from him, no purple-faced alcoholics with big mustaches. I will be accompanied by people of nobility who experience tranquility because they don't have to work for a living. I will be accompanied by mayors and great ones. I will be accompanied by people who can keep secrets, who are more likely to hit someone than say 'Put your hands up!' and to say 'Put your hands up!' than drink and to drink than pray. But I am not speaking entirely the truth. They pray to their country, or rather, they prey on their country. They ride up and down on her, and they walk on her. They treat her as if she were their boots, as well as their source of booty."

Gadshill exaggerated somewhat: He was expecting Prince Hal and Sir John to be members of his band of robbers, but most of the others were lowlifes without titles — and Sir John was a lowlife with a title.

"They treat their country as if she were their boots!" the chamberlain said. "Will she protect them from water when they walk on muddy roads?"

"She will, indeed," Gadshill said. "We have greased our way with bribes and made our boots waterproof. We steal in complete security, as if we were in a castle. It is as if we could walk invisibly, like the folk belief says about people who harvest invisible fern seeds and carry around a bag of them in their pockets."

"Don't put your trust in fern seeds," the chamberlain said. "Put your trust in darkness — it can better make you invisible."

"Shake hands with me," Gadshill said. "I promise as a honest man that you shall have a share in the booty because of the information you have given to me."

"I prefer that you promise as a false thief to give me a share of the booty," the chamberlain said.

"I am both an honest man and a dishonest thief — just not to the same people," Gadshill said. "I assume that you are the same. Tell the groom to get my gelding out of the stable. Farewell, you dumb joker."

On the road near Gads Hill, Prince Hal and Poins talked together. Peto and Bardolph were also present.

Poins said, "Let's hide ourselves. I have taken Falstaff's horse and hidden it from him, and now he is complaining. His nerves are fraying like cheap velvet."

Prince Hal said to the others, "Hide yourselves!"

They hid themselves in shrubbery.

Falstaff arrived and said, "Poins! Poins, damn you!"

Prince Hal said, "Be quiet, you fat-kidneyed rascal! What a racket you are making!"

"Where's Poins, Hal?" Falstaff asked.

"He walked up to the top of the hill. I'll go and seek him."

Prince Hal departed.

"I have been cursed — that must be why I rob in the company of Poins!" Falstaff said. "That scoundrel! He has taken my horse and hidden it somewhere — I don't know where! If I walk even four more feet, I will completely lose my breath. Well, I plan to die a good death despite all this current misery — provided I escape hanging for killing Poins. For every hour of the past twenty-two years, I have sworn to myself that I will drop him as one of my friends, but yet I enjoy his company. I swear that he must have given me a friendship potion."

Falstaff called, "Poins! Hal!"

No answer came back, and Falstaff said, "Damn you both!" He believed that Prince Hal must also be in on the practical joke.

Falstaff then called, "Bardolph! Peto!"

No answer came back, and Falstaff said, "I prefer to die rather than rob a foot further. Drink is a good thing, and I think that reforming myself and becoming an honest man — and leaving these rogues — would be as good as drink. If it isn't, then I am the worst scoundrel who ever chewed with a tooth. Walking eight yards of uneven ground on foot for me is the equivalent of walking seventy miles on foot for a person of normal weight. These stonyhearted villains know it well enough. The world must be damned if there is no honor among thieves."

Falstaff heard a whistle from the others.

He said, "Whew! A plague upon you all! Give me my horse, you rogues — give me my horse, and be hanged!"

Accompanied by Poins, Prince Hal walked up to Falstaff and said, "Be quiet, fat guts! Lie down; put your ear close to the ground and listen. You may be able to hear the tread of travelers."

Fat Falstaff replied, "Do you have any levers to lift me up again, after I lie down? I think not. I swear that I will not carry my own flesh so far on foot ever again — not even for all the money in your father's royal treasury! Why are you horsing around and playing a joke on me?"

"No horsing around can take place," Prince Hal said. "You don't have a horse."

"Please, Hal," Falstaff said. "Please, Prince, help me get my horse back."

Prince Hal replied, "Why should I help you get on your horse's back? I am not your groom."

Falstaff said, "Go and hang yourself in your own heir-apparent garters! After all, you are a member of the Order of the Garters. I swear, if I am caught robbing I will turn informant and get all of you arrested. I swear that I will have filthy ballads written about all of you and have them sung everywhere. If I don't, let a cup of sack be my poison — I will drink myself to death! This practical joke has gotten out of hand — and left me on foot! I hate it when the game is afoot and I happen to be the game."

Gadshill, Bardolph, and Peto showed up.

Gadshill joked, "Stand still and put your hands up!"

Falstaff replied, "I am standing — very much against my will."

Poins said, "I know who this is — I recognize his voice. This is Gadshill, who gets the information we need to rob people and who arranges the robbery."

Bardolph asked, "Gadshill, do you have any news for us?"

Gadshill replied, "Cover your faces. Put your masks on. Money that belongs to the King is coming down the hill. It's going to the King's treasury."

"That's a lie," Falstaff said. "It's going to the King's Tavern, one of my favorite drinking spots."

Gadshill said, "There's enough money to make us all."

Falstaff added, "To be hanged."

Prince Hal took charge. He and Poins stood close together. Prince Hal said to the others, "You four shall encounter them face to face in the narrow lane. Ned Poins and I will approach them from behind. If they flee from you, they will run into Poins and me."

Peto asked, "How many of them are there?"

"Some eight or ten," Gadshill replied.

"Damn!" Falstaff said. "Aren't they more likely to rob us than we are to rob them?"

"Are you a coward, Sir John Paunch?" Prince Hal asked.

"Indeed, I am not John of Gaunt, your grandfather," Falstaff replied, "but I am no coward, Hal."

"We will quickly put that to the test," Prince Hal said.

Poins said to Falstaff, "Your horse is behind that hedge. When you need your horse, that is where you will find him. Farewell. Be brave."

Poins and Prince Hal left.

Falstaff said, "I am so happy to get my horse back that I won't take revenge against Poins."

Hidden from the others, Prince Hal said to Poins, "Ned, where are our disguises?"

"Very near. I will take you to them."

As the others waited to rob the travelers, Falstaff said, "May happiness and success be our lot. Let each of us attend to our present business."

The four travelers arrived.

One traveler said, "Come, neighbor. The boy shall lead our horses down the hill. We will walk for a while and stretch our legs."

The thieves yelled, "Put your hands up!"

The travelers shouted, "Help!"

Falstaff yelled, "Kill them! Cut their throats! They're nothing but miserable parasites! They are fat, bacon-fed knaves! They hate young people like us. Down with them! Rob them!"

Falstaff, an old man, hoped that the travelers would tell the law officials that young men had robbed them.

In the confusion, the travelers kept shouting, "Help!"

Falstaff shouted, "Go hang yourselves, you potbellied knaves! Are you losing all that you own! I wish that was so! I wish that everything you owned were here so we could take it! You fat misers! You pork bellies! Young men must live, too! Aren't you the wealthy men who serve as grandjurors! We'll jure you — we'll injure you!"

The robbers tied up the four travelers and took their valuables and then departed.

Prince Hal and Poins had watched the robbery from a hidden place.

Prince Hal said to Poins, "The robbers have bound the honest men. If you and I can now rob the robbers and go merrily to London, we will have good conversation for a week, much laughter for a month, and the memory of a good jest forever."

They followed the thieves to catch up to them.

Poins said, "I can hear them now."

Falstaff said to Bardolph, Peto, and Gadshill, "Let's divvy up the loot and ride back to London before daybreak. Both Prince Hal and Poins are complete and utter cowards — we have seen plenty of proof of that! Poins has no more courage than can be found in a wild duck."

The thieves began to divide up the money.

Disguised and wearing masks, Prince Hal and Poins came forward, brandishing swords.

Disguising his voice, Prince Hal shouted, "Give us your money!"

Disguising his voice, Poins shouted, "Or die!"

The thieves ran away, including Falstaff, who screamed and lashed out with his sword once or twice before running away. The thieves left behind their booty.

"That was easy," Prince Hal said. "Now we will get happily on our horses. The thieves are all scattered and separated from each other. They are so overcome with fear that they dare not meet each other. Each of them will think that the others are officers of the law. Let's leave, good Ned. Falstaff sweats to death, and he waters the lean earth as he walks. If it weren't so funny, I would pity him."

Poins said, "How he roared with fright!"

Hotspur stood in a room in his home, Warkworth Castle in Northumberland, as he read a letter out loud.

Hotspur read, "For my part, my lord, I would be happy to be there because of the respect that I have for your family."

He said, "Then why won't you be there and be a part of our rebellion? He writes that he would be happy to be there, and yet he will not be there. This letter shows that he loves his own barn more than he loves the House of the Percys. Let me read some more."

Hotspur read, "The purpose you undertake is dangerous."

He said, "That is true: A rebellion against a King is dangerous. It can also be dangerous to catch a cold. People can die from that, and they can die in their sleep or while eating and drinking. If you were here, my lord fool, I would tell you that out of this nettle called danger, we will pluck a flower called safety."

Hotspur read, "The purpose you undertake is dangerous. The friends you have named are unreliable, the timing is poor, and your forces too light to defeat so great an opposition."

He said, "Do you really think so? If you were here, I would call you a shallow, cowardly menial servant, and I would tell you that you lie. What a lack-brain you are! By the Lord, our plot is as good a plot as ever was laid, and our friends are true and constant. We have a good plot and good friends, and we are full of expectations for victory. Yes, we have an excellent plot and very good friends. What a frosty-spirited rogue is this writer! Why, the Archbishop of York commends the plot and the general course of action. If I were now by the rascally writer of this letter, I could dash out his brains by merely hitting him with his lady's fan! Is there not my father, my uncle, and myself all joined together in this rebellion? And Lord Edmund Mortimer, the Archbishop of York, and Owen Glendower? Don't we also have on our side the Earl of Douglas? Haven't I received letters from all of them to meet me with their armies by the ninth of the next month? Haven't some of them already started their marches? This letter-writer has no faith! He is a pagan rascal! He is an infidel! Ha! Now he — fearful and with a cold heart — will go to the King and tell him about our rebellion. I could split myself in two and kick myself because

I contacted this dish of skim milk and tried to get him to join our honorable rebellion! Hang him! Let him tell the King! We are prepared. I will set out tonight to meet Glendower."

Hotspur's wife, Kate, entered the room. She was worried about her husband and her marriage.

Hotspur said to her, "How are you, Kate! I must leave you within the next two hours."

Kate replied, "My husband, why do you insist on being alone? For what offence have I for the past two weeks been banished from your bed? Tell me, Hotspur, what is it that is troubling you and takes from you your appetite, your pleasure, and your golden sleep? Why do you stare at the ground and why are you so easily startled when you sit by yourself? Why have you lost the ruddiness in your cheeks? Why have you ignored me and not had sex with me? You have not enjoyed my body and you have not allowed me to enjoy your body — a right I have as your wife. Why instead have you been staring at nothing and brooding? While you have slept — lightly, not deeply — I have crept to your bed and have listened to you talk in your sleep. You have murmured tales of iron wars. You have given your bounding steed orders. You have cried 'Courage' and 'To the battlefield!' And you have talked of sallies and retreats, of trenches and tents, of palisades made of stakes and of parapets made of stone and of other fortifications, of big and small cannon, of prisoners ransomed and of soldiers slain, and of all the occurrences of a violent fight. Your spirit has been so at war that you have thus fought battles in your sleep, and beads of sweat have stood upon your forehead like bubbles in a recently disturbed stream. And in your face strange expressions have appeared such as we see when men stop breathing when they hear suddenly a command of great importance. What portents are these? You are considering some serious business, and you must tell me what it is, or else I will know that you do not love me."

A servant entered the room and Hotspur asked him, "Has Gilliams departed with the packet of letters?"

"He has been gone for an hour," the servant replied.

"Has Butler brought those horses from the shire Sheriff?"

"He has just now brought one horse."

"Which horse? Was it a roan with cropped ears?"

"It is, my lord."

"That roan shall by my throne," Hotspur said. "Well, I will ride him immediately. The Percy family motto is '*Esperance*!' or 'Hope!' and that is what I have now. Tell Butler to take the roan into the park."

The servant departed.

Kate said, "Now listen here, husband."

"What have you got to say, wife?" Hotspur replied.

"What is it that carries you away?"

"Why, my horse, my love, my horse."

"Stop joking, you mad-headed ape!" Kate said. "Even a weasel is less annoying than you are right now. I swear that I will know your business, husband — that I will! I fear that my brother Mortimer is making a move to become King of England, and he wants you to fight on his behalf and strengthen his armies, but if you go —"

Hotspur joked, "So far afoot, I shall be weary, love."

Kate said, "Come, come, you parrot, give me the real answer to my question."

She grabbed the little finger of one of her husband's hands and threatened, charmingly, "I promise that I'll break your little finger, Harry, unless you tell me everything I want to know."

"Away, you trifler!" Hotspur said, not unkindly. "You talked of love. Love! I do not love you, Kate. This is no world to play with dolls and to duel with lips. We must have bloody noses and cracked crowns. That is the currency of our age. Now I must go to my horse!"

Kate grabbed onto Hotspur and did not let go.

Hotspur asked, "What's wrong, Kate?"

Hotspur had been joking when he had said that he did not love his wife, but for Kate this was serious business.

Upset, she said, "Do you not love me? Do you not, indeed? Is that true? If you do not love me, I will not love myself. Don't you love me? Tell me whether or not you were joking."

Hotspur replied, "Will you come with me and see me mount my horse? Once I am on horseback, I will swear to you that I love you always and forever. But, Kate, you must not ask me where I am going or what is the reason for my journey. I must go where I must go, and this evening, gentle Kate, I must leave you. I know that you are wise, but yet you are a wife. I know that you are loyal, but yet you are a woman. As for keeping a secret, no lady is more closed-mouthed than you — because I believe that you will not tell what you do not know. This is as far as I will trust you, Kate."

"Only that far?" a disappointed Kate said.

"And no further," Hotspur said. "But, Kate, I promise that you will go where I am going. Today, I will set out on the journey. Tomorrow, you will set out. Will that satisfy you, Kate?"

"It will have to."

They went to the park, where the roan horse was waiting.

Ned Poins was in a room in the Boar's-Head Tavern in Eastcheap.

Prince Hal entered a room of the Boar's-Head Tavern, saw Poins in another room, and called to him, "Ned! Come out of that hot room and laugh with me until Falstaff and the others arrive."

Poins entered the room that Prince Hal was in and asked, "Where have you been, Hal?"

Prince Hal answered, "I have been with three or four blockhead bartenders in the midst of sixty or eighty barrels of wine and ale in the cellar. I have been with some of the lowest members of the working class. Now I am a sworn brother to a trio of bartenders, and I can call them all by their Christian names: Tom, Dick, and Francis. They swear to God that, although I am only the Prince of Wales, yet I am the King of Courtesy. They tell me that I am not a Proud Jack like Falstaff. Instead, I am a Corinthian — a jolly drinking buddy — as well as a lad of mettle and a good man. That's what they call me. And they say that when I am King of England, all the good lads in Eastcheap will support me. In addition, they have been teaching me their lingo. They call drinking deep 'dyeing scarlet' because of the effect that alcoholism has on the color of the alcoholic's face. When someone pauses to breathe while chugging, they cry, 'Ahem!' and bid the drinker to finish off the drink.

"After spending just fifteen minutes with them, I am so proficient in their lingo that I can drink with any tinker using his own language throughout my life. I tell you, Ned, you have lost out by not being with me during this lesson. But, Ned, to sweeten your life, I give you this pennyworth of sugar, clapped just now into my hand by an apprentice bartender, one who has never spoken any words in his life other than those needed in his job as a bartender: 'Eight shillings and sixpence' and 'You are welcome' and 'Coming in a moment, sir' and 'Charge a pint of Spanish sweet wine in the Half-Moon Room' and so on.

"But, Ned, to pass the time until Falstaff comes, please stand in some neighboring room, while I question the young bartender who gave me the sugar about how I should use that sugar. Of course, I know that it is to be used to sweeten wine. While I talk to the bartender, you keep calling his name: Francis. This will confuse him and all his conversation will consist of 'Coming!' This will be funny now and set the tone for the fun we will have at Falstaff's expense later."

Poins went into a neighboring room and called, "Francis!"

"That's perfect," Prince Hal said to Poins.

Francis entered the room Prince Hal was in. He called, "Coming!" to Poins, and to a bartender in the room he had just left he called, "Look after the Pomegranate Room, Ralph."

Prince Hal said, "Come here, Francis."

"Yes, my lord. What do you need?" Francis replied.

"How long have you been an apprentice bartender, Francis?"

"Two years, so I have five more years of apprenticeship to serve, and —"

Poins called from the other room, "Francis!"

"Coming!" Francis called back.

"Two years, and five more years to go!" Prince Hal said. "That's a long apprenticeship for the clinking of pewter mugs! Francis, could you be so brave a person as to be a coward when it comes to your apprenticeship and run away from it?"

"I swear on all the Bibles in England that I —"

"Francis!" Poins called.

"Coming, sir!" Francis called.

"How old are you, Francis?" Prince Hal asked.

"Let's see. At the next Michaelmas — September 29th — I will be —"

"Francis!" Poins called.

"Coming, sir!" Francis called. To Prince Hal, he asked, "Can you wait a moment, sir, and let me take care of that customer?"

Prince Hal replied, "No, but listen, Francis, the sugar you gave me was a penny's worth, wasn't it?"

"Lord, I wish that it had been worth two pennies!"

"In return for it, I will give you a thousand pounds," Prince Hal said. "Ask for it whenever you want it, and you shall get it."

"Francis!" Poins called.

"At once, sir!" Francis called to Poins.

"You want the thousand pounds at once, Francis?" Prince Hal said. "No, Francis. Not at once, Francis. But tomorrow, Francis; or, Francis, on Thursday; or indeed, Francis, whenever you want it. But, Francis —"

"Yes, my lord?"

Prince Hal said, "If you run away from your apprenticeship, you will rob a leather-jacket-with-crystal-buttons-wearing, short-haired, agate-ring-wearing, wool-socks-with-plain-garters-wearing, unctuous-speaking man with a money pouch of Spanish leather."

Prince Hal was describing the owner of the tavern, who would lose financially if Francis did not serve the remainder of his apprenticeship. Although not in plain words, Prince Hal was hinting to Francis that if he left his master, then Prince Hal would find a place for him at the King's palace. Such a place would greatly improve Francis' life — and so be worth at least figuratively a thousand pounds. All Francis had to do was to be clever enough to know what Prince Hal was offering him and to say that yes, he was willing to run away from his master and apprenticeship and to take action to improve his life.

Unfortunately, Francis asked, "Sir, who do you mean?"

"If you don't know who I mean, then you are doomed to have wine stain your white shirts," Prince Hal said.

He added, "In Barbary, sir, it cannot come to so much."

By this, Prince Hal meant that in Barbary — or anywhere but here and now — a penny's worth of sugar would not be worth a thousand pounds or a life-changing job.

Francis, who — like most of us — was not clever enough to respond the right way to Prince Hal's semi-doubletalk, merely asked, "What, sir?"

"Francis!" Poins called.

"Go, Francis," Prince Hal said. "Don't you hear him calling you?"

At the same time, both Prince Hal and Poins called, "Francis!"

Francis stood, mouth open, not knowing what to do.

Francis' master, the innkeeper, entered the room that Prince Hal and Francis were in and said, "Francis, why are you standing still and doing nothing when so many customers are calling you? Go and do your job."

Francis departed.

The innkeeper then said to Prince Hal, "My lord, old Sir John Falstaff, with half-a-dozen more men, are at the door. Shall I let them in?"

Prince Hal replied, "Let them wait for a few more minutes. I will let you know when to open the door to them."

The innkeeper departed, and Prince Hal called, "Poins."

Poins entered the room, saying, as Francis so often did, "Coming, sir!"

Prince Hal said, "Falstaff and the rest of the thieves are at the door. Are we ready to laugh at them?"

"We shall be as merry as grasshoppers in the summer," Poins said. "But what was the point of your jesting with Francis?"

"The jest with Francis served as the prologue to the upcoming jest with Falstaff," Prince Hal said. "I am now in the mood for humor although I am also ready for any other mood. Jests have been played since the old days of Adam and Eve until this present time: right now at midnight."

Prince Hal thought, *I am in the mood for humor, but I realize that many, many people lack the leisure or the temperament for humor. Some people are over-burdened by work and are unable to participate in fun even when it would be advantageous for them to do so.*

Francis re-entered the room carrying a bottle of wine.

Prince Hal asked him, "What time is it?"

Francs ignored Prince Hal and said, "Coming, sir!" He left the room.

Prince Hal said, "I am amazed that this apprentice bartender should speak fewer words than a parrot and yet he is the son of a woman! His life consists only of running downstairs to get wine and running upstairs to serve it. His conversation consists only of telling customers the size of their bar bills."

Prince Hal thought of a person whose life resembled Francis' in being single-sided. Francis' life consisted of work. Hotspur's life consisted of seeking glory and honor. Neither seemed to have any time for fun or to value it.

Prince Hal said, "My mind is not yet like the mind of Hotspur of the north. Hotspur kills some six or seven dozen Scots during breakfast, washes his hands, and says to his wife, 'I hate this quiet life! I want work.' She replies, 'Oh, my sweet Harry, how many have you killed today?' Hotspur says, 'Give my roan horse a medicinal drink,' and then answers his wife, 'Approximately fourteen.' An hour later, he calls the number 'a trifle, a trifle.'"

Prince Hal thought, *Francis and Hotspur are different in one way. Francis works all the time. Hotspur would like more work — he would like more battles in which to kill people.*

He also thought, *I am getting an education about the lower classes. I know a lot about the lowlifes who are robbers: the criminal lower class. Now I know more about the working lower class. Francis is a blockhead, but no wonder — all his time is filled with work. He will be an apprentice for seven years in a job that should require very little time to master. I am fortunate in that I have time for leisure and fun.*

Prince Hal then called to the innkeeper, "Please, let Falstaff in."

He then said to Poins, "We will have a play extempore. I'll play Percy, and that damned fat boar Falstaff shall play Hotspur's wife."

He looked at the entrance to the room and added, "'Yahoo!' says the drunkard. Here comes Sir Ribs! Here comes Sir Tallow."

Falstaff, Gadshill, Bardolph, and Peto entered the room. Francis followed them, bringing wine.

Poins said, "Welcome, Jack. Where have you been?"

Falstaff replied, "A plague on all cowards, I say — make that a plague and a vengeance, too! Amen to that! Give me a cup of sack, Francis. Before I lead this life any longer, I'll sew stockings and mend them and make new bottoms for them, too. A plague on all cowards! Give me a cup of sack, Francis. Isn't anyone courageous any more?"

Prince Hal said to Poins, "Have you ever seen the Sun, sometimes called Titan by Homer in mythology, kiss a dish of butter? The butter melts and flows just like the wine that is flowing down Falstaff's throat. Look at Falstaff right now, and you will see the Sun kiss a dish of butter. Falstaff is the Sun, and the sack is the butter that is melting into nothingness."

Falstaff chugged the wine and then said to Francis, "You rogue, there's lime in this sack! You added the lime to bad wine to make it seem to be better than it is! Men are villains and rogues and cheats, but a coward is worse than a cup of sack with lime in it. A villainous coward! You may as well end your days and die, old Jack, because manhood, good manhood, has been forgotten upon the face of the earth. If it has not, then I am as skinny as a pole. There live not three good men unhanged in England, and one of them is fat and grows old. God help us all in these bad times! We live in a bad world, I say. I wish I were a Puritan weaver so I could sing psalms at my work. And still I say this: a plague on all cowards!"

"Weaver, huh?" Prince Hal said. "What's wrong, you huge bale of wool? What are you muttering about?"

"A King's son, huh?" Falstaff said. "I really ought to get myself a theatrical prop that looks like a dagger and drive you out of the kingdom like the Devil is driven away in old religious plays. While I'm at it, I ought to drive all of your subjects before you like a flock of wild geese! In fact, if I don't do that, I swear never again to wear hair on my face. You call yourself the Prince of Wales!"

Prince Hal replied, "Why, you fat son of a whore, what's the matter?"

"Are you not a coward?" Falstaff asked. "Answer me that. And is not Poins there also a coward?"

Poins said, "By God, you fat paunch, if you call me a coward, I'll stab you."

"Am I calling you a coward?" Falstaff said. "No, I am not calling you a coward, but — damn you! — I would give a thousand pounds if I could run as fast as you can. You have good posture — you must because you don't care who sees your back. Do you call what you did backing up your friends? A plague on such backing! Give me friends who will stand face forward and not turn their backs. Give me a cup of sack — I am a rogue if I have drunk today."

Francis handed him a cup of sack.

"Liar!" Prince Hal said. "Your lips are scarcely wiped since the last time you drank!"

"Yes, and so what?" Falstaff replied.

He drank deeply, and then he said, "I still say this: A plague on all cowards!"

"What's wrong?" Prince Hal asked.

"What's wrong!" Falstaff said. "Four of us here stole a thousand pounds early this morning."

"Where is it, Jack?" Prince Hal asked. "Where is it?"

"Where is it! Taken from us it was! A hundred men set upon the poor four of us."

Prince Hal pretended to be surprised and exclaimed, "What, a hundred men?"

"I am a rogue, if I were not fighting at close quarters with a dozen of them for two hours. I have escaped only by a miracle. Their swords cut through my shirt eight times and through my trousers four times. My shield has been pierced again and again; my sword is hacked like a handsaw — look at it!"

Falstaff raised his sword so that Prince Hal and Poins could look at its edge, which was jagged as if it had been used in fighting, and then he said, "I never fought better since I became a man, but even my best was not enough. A plague on all cowards!"

Falstaff pointed to Peto and Gadshill and said, "Let them speak: If they speak more or less than the truth, and anything but the truth, they are lowlifes and the sons of darkness."

Prince Hal asked, "Speak, sirs. What happened?"

Gadshill began to speak, "We four men set upon some dozen —"

Falstaff interrupted, "Sixteen at least."

Gadshill continued, "And bound them."

Peto said, "No, no, they were not bound."

Falstaff interrupted, "You rogue, they were bound, every man of them. If they were not, then I am a Jew — a Hebrew Jew."

Gadshill continued, "As we were divvying the money, some six or seven fresh men set upon us —"

Falstaff interrupted, "And unbound the rest, and then in came some other men."

Prince Hal asked, "What, fought you with them all?"

Falstaff replied, "All! I know not what you call all; but if I fought with fewer than fifty of them, I am as skinny as spaghetti. If fifty-two or fifty-three people did not fight poor fat old me, then I walk on four legs and not two."

Prince Hal said, "Pray to God that you did not murder any of them."

"It's too late to pray for that," Falstaff replied. "I made it hot for two of them. They have died and gone to Hell. I am sure that two of them are roasting: two rogues in buckram suits. I tell you what, Hal, if I tell you a lie, spit in my face and call me a stupid horse."

Falstaff continued, "You know my style of fighting." He assumed a fencing position and added, "Like this I stood and thus I bore my sword. Four rogues in buckram attacked me —"

"What, four?" Prince Hal said. "You said there were but two just now."

"Four, Hal," Falstaff replied. "I told you four."

To encourage Falstaff to continue lying, Poins took his side: "True. He said four."

"These four attacked me and mightily thrust their swords at me. I did not panic but took the points of their seven swords in my shield."

"Seven men attacked you?" Prince Hal said. "There were just four a moment ago."

"In buckram?" Falstaff asked.

Ned Poins said, "Yes, four, in buckram suits."

"Seven," Falstaff said. "I swear by the hilts that form a cross on my sword, or I am a villain else."

Prince Hal said, "Ned, let him alone. We shall hear about even more fighters soon."

"Did you hear me, Hal?" Falstaff asked.

"Not only did I hear you, but I am keeping count, too," Prince Hal replied.

"My tale is well worth paying attention to," Falstaff said. "These nine fighters in buckram that I told you about —"

"See, two more already," Prince Hal said to Poins.

"The points of their swords broke against my shield —"

"And they were so afraid they peed their pants," Poins said.

"They began to back away from me," Falstaff continued. "I followed them closely, attacked, and as quickly as thought I stabbed seven of the eleven of them."

Prince Hal exclaimed, "How monstrous! Eleven men in buckram grown out of two!"

Falstaff continued, "But, as the Devil would have it, three misbegotten knaves wearing Kendal green outfits came at my back and let drive at me; for it was so dark, Hal, that you could not even see your hand."

"These lies are like their father who begets them: huge as a mountain and obvious and easily perceived," Prince Hal said to Poins.

He said to Falstaff, "Why, you clay-brained guts, you blockheaded fool, you son of a whore, you obscene pan that that catches the drippings of grease from a roasted bird —"

"What's wrong?" Falstaff asked. "Are you insane? Is not the truth the truth?"

Prince Hal asked, "Why, how could you know that these men were wearing Kendal green, when it was so dark that you could not see your hand? Come on and tell us how you knew. What do you have to say, Jack?"

"Yes, Jack," Poins said, "Tell us how you knew."

"You forgot to say 'please,'" Falstaff said. "I will not answer the questions of any men who forget to say 'please' — I will not answer their questions even if I were being tortured on the rack or if my hands were tied behind me and then I was lifted into the air by my hands. I would not answer your question even if you said 'please' now — it's too late! Give you an answer without you saying 'please' — I think not. I am offended by your lack of courtesy, really I am. I will not answer questions upon compulsion."

Prince Hal said, "I will be no longer guilty of this sin. You are a bloody coward! You are a breaker of beds! You are a breaker of horses' backs! You are a huge hill of flesh!"

Falstaff gave as good as he got — and more: "You are a starveling! You are the skin of an eel! You are the tongue of an ox! You are the penis of a bull! You are a long, skinny, dried codfish! I wish that I had more breath so that I could mention everything that you resemble! You are the yardstick of a tailor! You are the sheath of a sword! You are the case of a violin bow! You are a vile upright rapier!"

Falstaff started to gasp for breath.

Prince Hal said, "Catch your breath, and then again make your comparisons. When you have tired of comparing me to long, skinny objects, then listen to what I have to say."

He waited a moment, but Falstaff continued to breathe heavily.

Poins said, "Listen carefully, Jack."

Prince Hal said, "Poins and I saw you, Gadshill, Peto, and Bardolph rob four travelers and tie them up. You had all their money. Listen to the truth about what happened thereafter. Poins and I attacked you — not with swords but with a few words. You cowards ran away, and we took the money. We have it, and we can show it to you in this inn. And, Falstaff, you carried your guts away as nimbly, with as quick dexterity, and roared for mercy and still ran and roared, as ever I heard a bull calf run and bellow. What a base joker you are to hack up your sword as you have done, and then say your sword was damaged in a fight! Now, explain yourself. What trick, what device, what hiding-place can you now find that will protect you from your obvious and apparent shame?"

"Come, Jack," Poins said. "Speak up. What do you have to say for yourself?"

Falstaff replied, "With God as my witness, I say that I knew you as well as He Who made you! I knew that the men who robbed us were you two the whole time!"

He turned to Prince Hal and said, "Was I going to kill the heir apparent? Was I going to attack the true Prince? Of course not! Why, you know that I am as brave as Hercules, but instinct prevails. According to legend, the lion will not harm the true Prince. Instinct is a great matter; I was a coward by instinct. I shall think the better of both of us during my life. I am a valiant lion, and you are a true Prince. But, by the Lord, lads, I am glad you have the money!"

Falstaff then tried to change the subject. He turned to a doorway and shouted, "Hostess, shut the doors. We will party late tonight, and then pray tomorrow."

The Hostess heard him and went to shut the doors.

Falstaff then said to everyone, "Gallants, lads, boys, hearts of gold, all the titles of good fellowship come to you! Shall we be merry? Shall we have a play extempore?"

"Good idea," Prince Hal said, "and the topic of the play shall be your running away in fear."

"Let us hear no more about that, Hal," Falstaff said, "if you are my friend."

The Hostess entered the room and said, "Prince Hal, there is trouble."

Prince Hal replied, "Hostess, what is going on?"

"My lord, there is a nobleman of the court at the door who wishes to speak with you. He says that he comes from your father the King."

Prince Hal did not want to talk to him: "He is a noble, and a noble is worth six shillings and eight pence. Give him a royal, which is worth ten shillings. That will make him a royal man, and you can send him to my mother without his talking to me."

Falstaff knew that Prince Hal's mother was dead and that he wanted to get rid of the nobleman without speaking to him.

Falstaff asked, "What kind of man is he?"

The Hostess replied, "An old man."

"I wonder what an old man is doing out of bed so late at night. It's midnight," Falstaff said. He asked Prince Hal, "Shall I talk to him?"

"Please do, Jack," Prince Hal said.

"I'll send him packing," Falstaff promised. He left the room.

Prince Hal said to Gadshill, "You fought well."

He added, "So did you, Peto, and so did you, Bardolph. You are lions, too. You also ran away by instinct — you will not touch the true Prince."

Bardolph said, "I ran when I saw others run."

Prince Hal asked, "Tell me the truth. How did Falstaff's sword come to be so hacked up?"

Peto replied, "He hacked it with his dagger, and he swore that he would make you believe it was done in a fight — in fact, he said that he would swear his lies so strongly that truth would be banished from England — and he persuaded us to do the same thing."

"That he did," Bardolph said. "He persuaded us to tickle our noses with spear-grass to make them bleed, and then to beslubber our garments with the blood and swear that it was the blood of true men. I did something that I have not done for seven years: I blushed to hear his monstrous devices."

"Liar!" Prince Hal said, looking at Bardolph's face, which was red from his alcoholism and scarred and marred from pimples and pustules and carbuncles and boils. "You stole a cup of sack eighteen years ago, and were caught and so blushed. Ever since, you have drunk sack and acquired a permanent blush. Most people are caught red-handed; you were caught red-complexioned.

"But, Bardolph, you had the fire of your face and you had your sword, and yet you ran away. What instinct of yours made you do that?"

Bardolph pointed to his own face and said, "My lord, do you see these flaming-red meteors that I have had for a long time? Meteors often predict the future."

"I do see them," Prince Hal said.

"What then-coming events do you think they were evidence of?" Bardolph asked.

"A liver grown hot and a wallet grown empty because of alcoholism," Prince Hal answered.

"The correct answer, my lord, is choler, or an angry temperament. I am no coward," Bardolph said.

"Given your profession and your alcoholism, I think that they are predicting a collar," Prince Hal replied. "You will be collared by the officers of the law, and most likely after that you will wear a different kind of collar — a halter, also known as a hangman's noose."

Falstaff entered the room.

Prince Hal said, "Here comes lean Jack, here comes bare-bone. How are you, my sweet creature of cotton padding and high-sounding nonsense! How long ago has it been, Jack, since you last saw your own knees?"

"My own knees!" Falstaff said. "Why, when I was about your age, Hal, I was not as large as an eagle's talon in the waist. I could have slipped into any alderman's thumb-ring and worn it as a belt. A plague on sighing and grief — it blows a man's waist up like a balloon!"

He added, "There's villainous news abroad. The old man at the door was Sir John Bracy, who was sent by your father. You must go to the palace in the morning. There is trouble from that mad fellow of the north, Hotspur, and from the magician of Wales, he who beat with a club the Devil named Amamon and made horns grow on Lucifer by cuckolding him and forced the Devil to swear to be his servant upon the cross of a Welsh hook — which does not have a cross. What is his name?"

Poins said, "Glendower."

"Owen Glendower," Falstaff said. "Yes, that is his name. Also causing trouble is his son-in-law Mortimer, and the old Earl of Northumberland, and that sprightly Scot of Scots: the Earl of Douglas, who runs on horseback up a hill perpendicularly."

Prince Hal said, "Douglas: He who is supposed to ride at high speed and with his pistol kill a flying sparrow."

"You have hit the nail on the head," Falstaff said.

"He never hit the sparrow in the head," Prince Hal replied.

"Douglas has good metal in his bullets and good mettle — courage — in himself," Falstaff said. "He will not run."

"Didn't you just say that he runs on horseback up a hill perpendicularly?" Prince Hal asked.

Falstaff said, "You are acting like a cuckoo when you repeat my words without distinguishing their meaning. Douglas will run — ride fast — on horseback. But he will not run — flee in fear — on foot. Is this clear? He will run on horseback, but on foot he will not budge an inch. On foot he will not run away."

"Yes, he will," Prince Hal, who was still in a mood for humor, said. "He will run away by instinct."

Falstaff shrugged and said, "Fair enough. He will run by instinct. Anyway, Douglas is causing trouble, as are Mordake and a thousand Scots. People are rebelling against your father the King. The Earl of Worcester is part of the rebellion. He has gone to Wales to meet Glendower. Your father's beard has turned white with the news. People are worried: You may buy land now as cheap as stinking mackerel. In times of war, people sell cheap what they are afraid they will lose."

Growing serious, Prince Hal said, "It is likely if we still have civil war this coming June, we shall buy maidenheads as carpenters buy hobnails, by the hundreds. Women and girls will be selling their bodies so that they can buy food."

For Falstaff, this was not a dismal prospect: "By God, Hal, that is true. It is likely that we shall have good trading that way."

Falstaff added, "Tell me, Hal. Aren't you horribly afraid? You are the heir apparent. Could anyone pick three worst enemies for you to fight than the fiend Douglas, the brave Hotspur, and that Devil Glendower? Aren't you horribly afraid? Doesn't your blood grow cold with fear?"

Prince Hal answered honestly, "No. I lack some of your instinct."

"When you see your father tomorrow, you will have to face his anger," Falstaff said. "Here's an idea: Why don't we rehearse that meeting so that you can practice what you will say?"

"Good idea," Prince Hal said. "You pretend to be my father the King. Ask me questions about how I am living my life."

"Shall I?" Falstaff, who was very willing to play that part in a play, asked. "Yes. This chair shall be my throne, this dagger shall be my scepter, and this cushion shall be my crown."

"Understood," Prince Hal said. "Your throne is a chair in a tavern, your golden scepter is a lead dagger, and your precious rich crown is a pitiful bald crown."

"If virtue is not completely absent from you, you shall now be moved," Falstaff said. "Give me a cup of sack to make my eyes look red, so that it may be thought I have wept — I must speak with deep emotion, and I will do it in King Cambyses' vein with lots of ranting and raving like the bombastic character in Thomas Preston's bombastic old play."

"Allow me to bow to you," Prince Hal said, and he bowed.

"And allow me to speak," Falstaff said. He asked his audience in the bar to give him a little room: "Stand aside, nobility."

The Hostess laughed at being called a member of nobility and said, "Oh, Falstaff is so funny!"

Falstaff said to her, "Weep not, sweet Queen; for trickling tears are vain."

The Hostess laughed and said, "I don't see how he can keep a straight face!"

Falstaff said, "Lords, escort my tristful Queen a few steps away for tears do fill the flood-gates of her eyes."

The Hostess said, "Oh, he does this character just like one of those rascally real actors!"

"Quiet, my little pot of ale. Quiet, my little Queen with the booze-tickled brain," Falstaff said to the Hostess.

To Prince Hal, he said, "Harry, I am amazed not only by where you spend your time but also by the company you keep. The more the chamomile plant is trodden down, the faster it grows, but the more youth is wasted, the quicker it disappears. That you are my son, I have partly your mother's word, partly my own opinion, but chiefly an evil glint in your eye and a silly-looking droop of your lower lip, both of which you inherited from me. If you are my son, then why, since you are my son, are you so gossiped about and criticized? Shall you, the blessed son of the King, turn out to be a truant and eat blackberries instead of doing your work? This question should not be asked of any heir apparent. Shall the son of the King turn out to be a thief and steal wallets? This question must be asked of this particular heir apparent: you. There is a thing, Harry, that you have often heard of — many in our land know it by the name of pitch, or sticky tar. This pitch, as many ancient writers have stated, makes people dirty — and so does the company you keep, Harry. I am speaking to you now, Harry, not befuddled by alcohol but as one who is weeping, not in pleasure but in sorrow, not just with words but also with woes. Yet, Harry, I have often noticed near you a virtuous man, but I don't know his name."

"Describe him to me, please, your majesty," Prince Hal requested.

"He is a handsome, portly man," Falstaff said. "He is portly in the sense of being stately — and fat. He has a cheerful look, a pleasing eye, and a most noble way of carrying himself. And I think his age is around fifty."

Falstaff's audience laughed. Falstaff was much more than fifty years old.

Falstaff continued, "Or perhaps sixty years old. Ah, now I remember — his name is Falstaff. If that man should be evilly inclined, Harry, I am deceived, for I see virtue in his looks. If the tree may be known by the fruit, as the fruit is known by the tree, then — emphatically I say it — there is virtue in that man. Keep him as your friend, and banish all the rest from your presence. Now, Harry, you naughty boy, tell me where you have been for the past month."

"Do you think that you sound like my father the King?" Prince Hal said. "Let's switch roles. You play me, and I will play my father."

"Are you deposing me?" Falstaff joked. "If you play the King half as well and half as majestically as I did, both in word and bearing, then hang me up by my heels like a baby rabbit sold by a man who sells chicken carcasses."

Prince Hal sat in the chair and said, "I am ready."

"As am I," Falstaff said. "Members of the audience, judge which of us is the better actor."

Prince Hal said, "Harry, from where have you come?"

"My noble lord, from Eastcheap," Falstaff replied.

"The complaints I hear about you are grievous."

"My lord, they are lies," Falstaff said to Prince Hal.

To the members of the audience, Falstaff said, "I will play a young Prince who will amuse you."

"Can you really swear to that, you profane boy?" Prince Hal asked. "From here on, never see me again. You are violently being turned away from all that is good. A Devil who has taken on the appearance of an old fat man is haunting you; your companion is an alcoholic barrel of a man. Why do you talk with that trunk of diseases, that bin of beastliness, that swollen parcel of bodily fluids, that huge jug of sack, that carrying case of guts, that Essex roasted ox with stuffing in its belly, that ancient figure of Vice who leads people into immorality, that grey-haired corrupter of youth, that father ruffian, that aged vanity?"

Prince Hal paused, and then he continued, "For what is he good, but to taste sack and drink it? In which activity is he neat and skillful, but to carve a chicken and eat it? In what is he skillful and cunning, but in crafty deceit? In what is he crafty, but in villainy? In what is he villainous, but in all things? In what is he worthy, but in nothing?"

Falstaff replied, "I do not understand you, my lord. Please explain."

"I am talking about that villainous abominable misleader of youth," Prince Hal said. "He is named Falstaff, and he is an old, white-bearded Satan."

"My lord, this man I know," Falstaff said.

"I know you do," Prince Hall said.

"But to say I know more harm in him than in myself, would be to say more than I know," Falstaff said.

This line got a big laugh from everyone except Prince Hal.

Falstaff continued, "It is true that he is old, but that is to be pitied — his white hairs do witness that he is old. But to say that he is — I beg your pardon for my language — a whoremaster, that is something I utterly deny. If drinking sack and sugar is a fault, God help the wicked! If to be old and merry is a sin, then many an old host whom I know is damned. If to be fat is to be hated, then the Egyptian Pharaoh's seven lean cattle that prophesied seven years of famine in his dream are to be loved. No, my good lord; banish Peto, banish Bardolph, banish Poins. But sweet Jack Falstaff, kind Jack Falstaff, true Jack Falstaff, valiant Jack Falstaff, and therefore more valiant, being, as he is, old Jack Falstaff, do not banish him from your Harry's company because if you banish plump Jack, then you banish all the world."

Prince Hal said coldly, "I do. I will."

A very loud knocking at the door interrupted the play. The Hostess, Francis, and Bardolph went to see who was knocking.

A panicked Bardolph quickly came running into the room where the impromptu play was being held.

Bardolph said to Prince Hal, "Oh, my lord! The Sheriff and several officers of the law are at the door!"

Falstaff wanted to continue the play. He yelled at Bardolph, "Out, you rogue! Let us finish the play: I have much to say on behalf of Falstaff."

The panicked Hostess entered the room but could say only, "My lord!"

An unpanicked Prince Hal asked the Hostess, "What's the matter? What mischief is afoot?"

"The Sheriff and lots of officers of the law are at the door. They have come to search the house. Shall I let them in?"

Hearing that, Falstaff was able to guess immediately why they wanted to search the inn: They were searching for evidence that would convict — and hang — the men who had robbed the travelers of 300 marks.

Falstaff said, "Did you hear that, Hal? What are you going to do? A true piece of gold should never be called a counterfeit. Despite some appearances to the contrary, you are true to your friends and would not turn your friends over to officers of the law so that they can be hanged."

In the play, Prince Hal had spoken the truth about Falstaff being a corrupter of youth, and he was half-tempted to let Falstaff hang. He said, "You, Falstaff, are a coward by nature, and not by instinct."

"I deny that I am a coward by nature, although I do not deny that I am a coward by instinct," Falstaff said. "If you will not let the Sheriff in and so keep him from arresting me, fine. But if you want to let the Sheriff in so that he can arrest me, that is also fine. I can be drawn in a cart to the gallows as well as any other man. Perhaps that has always been my future. I can hang as well as another man."

Prince Hal decided to be merciful. He ordered, "Falstaff, hide yourself in the little alcove hidden by that wall hanging. All of the rest of you, go upstairs so that you are not seen. Now all of us need honest faces and good consciences."

"I used to have those two things, but that was long ago," Falstaff said. "Therefore, I will hide."

Because the Hostess was still panicked, Prince Hal said to Peto, "Let the Sheriff in."

Peto opened the door and let in the Sheriff, one of the travelers who had been robbed, and some officers of the law. The traveler did not recognize Peto, who had worn a mask during the robbery.

Prince Hal, whom the Sheriff recognized, asked politely, "How can I help you?"

"First, pardon me, my lord," the Sheriff said. "We are searching for the men who robbed four travelers recently. Information that we have received has led us to this inn, where we think we will find the men we are seeking."

"Which men are they?" Prince Hal asked.

The Sheriff replied, "One of them is well known, my gracious lord. He is a massively fat man."

The traveler said, "As fat as butter."

Prince Hal replied, "I know the man you mean, but he is not here. I myself have employed the man on an errand."

This was true, equivocally. Falstaff was not in the room itself, but he was in an alcove in a wall of the room. And Prince Hal had ordered Falstaff to hide, so Falstaff's errand was to stay hidden until the Sheriff had left.

Prince Hal continued, "Sheriff, I give you my word that by noon tomorrow I will send him to you so that he can be questioned about anything he is accused of doing. And now let me ask you to leave this inn."

The heir apparent was a person to be obeyed. The Sheriff said, "I will, my lord."

But he added, "Four men have been robbed, two of whom — gentlemen — lost three hundred marks in the robbery."

"I don't doubt you," Prince Hal said. "If the fat man has robbed these men, he shall pay the penalty. And now, farewell."

"Good night, my noble lord," the Sheriff said.

"I think it is early morning, isn't it?" Prince Hal asked.

"Yes, my lord," the Sheriff replied. "I think it is two o'clock."

The Sheriff, the traveler, and the officers of the law departed, leaving behind Prince Hal and Peto.

Prince Hal said to Peto, "This oily rascal Falstaff is as well known as St. Paul's Cathedral. Go and call him."

Peto called, "Falstaff!"

He lifted the wall hanging, looked at Falstaff, and said, "He is fast asleep, and snorting like a horse."

Prince Hal listened and said, "He snores heavily. He is so fat that he works hard to draw in each breath."

He then said to Peto, "Search his pockets."

Peto followed Prince Hal's order.

"What did you find?"

"Nothing but papers, my lord."

"Let's see what they are. Read one of them to me."

Peto said, "Here is a tavern bill:

"*Item, A chicken, 2 shillings, 2 pence.*

"*Item, Sauce, 4 pence.*

"*Item, Sack, two gallons, 5 shillings, 8 pence.*

"*Item, Anchovies and sack after supper, 2 shillings, 6 pence.*

"*Item, Bread, a half-penny's worth.*

"That's monstrous!" Prince Hal said. "Only a half-penny's worth of bread to soak up so much wine! Keep all of Falstaff's papers. We will read them later. We will let Falstaff sleep. In the morning, I will go to the palace. All of us must go and fight in the war. Peto, I will find a position in the army for you that shall be honorable. I will put this fat rogue Falstaff in charge of a company of foot soldiers, although I think that he will die if he walks 240 yards. The money that all of you stole will be paid back with interest. I will see you again after I see my father. And so, good morning, Peto."

"Good morning, my lord," Peto said.

They departed.

CHAPTER 3

— 3.1 —

At Owen Glendower's castle in Wales, Hotspur, Worcester, Mortimer, and Glendower were holding a meeting.

Mortimer said, "The promises that we have made to each other are fair, the parties in our rebellion are sure, and the beginning of this, our rebellion, is full of promise and hope."

Hotspur said, "Lord Mortimer, and friend Glendower, will you sit down? And you, too, uncle Worcester."

By saying that, Hotspur was breaking a rule of etiquette. The castle belonged to Glendower, so Glendower — the host — should have been the one to invite the others to sit down.

Hotspur then said, "A plague upon it! I have forgotten the map!"

Glendower was better prepared than Hotspur. He said, "No, here it is. Sit, Earl of Worcester; sit, good Hotspur."

He paid Hotspur a compliment, "Whenever King Henry IV, the former Duke of Lancaster, says the name Hotspur, his cheek looks pale and with a heavy sigh he wishes that you were dead and in Heaven. The King of England is afraid of you."

Hotspur returned the compliment: "And whenever the King hears your name, he wishes that you were in Hell."

Glendower, who believed that he had been born to do great things, replied, "I cannot blame him. When I was born, the sky was full of the fiery shapes of burning meteors, and earthquakes made the foundation of the Earth shake like a coward."

Hotspur, who lacked the skills of diplomacy as well as the skills of etiquette, was unimpressed: "Why, so the Earth would have done at the same time, if your mother's cat had but given birth to kittens, even though you yourself had never been born."

Glendower was angry: "I say the Earth did shake when I was born."

"And I say the Earth was not of my mind, if you suppose that the Earth shook because it feared you," Hotspur replied.

"The Heavens were all on fire, and the Earth did tremble," Glendower said.

"In that case, the Earth trembled because the Heavens were all on fire, and not in fear of your birth," Hotspur said. "Nature can become ill; that illness is expressed in earthquakes. The Earth sometimes gets gas trapped inside it, and when it releases the gas it shakes so hard that steeples and moss-grown towers fall down. When you were born, the Earth let out a massive fart."

Glendower said, "Hotspur, I do not bear such insults from many men. Let me tell you again that when I was born the sky was full of fiery shapes, the goats ran from the mountains, and herds of cattle bellowed with fright in the fields. These signs have marked me out as extraordinary, and all the events of my life do show that I am not in the roll of common men. No man in England, Scotland, and Wales has ever taught me anything or had me as a pupil. No man is my master. And show me anyone who knows as much about magic as I do or can keep pace with me in my occult experiments."

Hotspur said to Mortimer and Worcester, "I think there's no man who speaks better Welsh than Glendower. No man speaks better nonsense. I think I'll go and eat dinner."

Mortimer said, "Please, brother-in-law Hotspur, don't make Glendower angry."

Too late. Glendower was angry.

Glendower said, "I can call spirits from the vast and deep underworld."

"Why, so can I, and so can any man," Hotspur said, "but will they come when you call them?"

"Why, I can teach you, Hotspur, to command the Devil."

"And I can teach you, Glendower, to shame the Devil by telling the truth. If you tell the truth, you will shame the Devil. So, if you have the power to raise the Devil, bring him here. I swear that I have the power to shame him and make him leave. Oh, while you live, tell the truth and shame the Devil!"

Mortimer said, "Stop! Let's have no more of these argumentative words."

Glendower continued to speak: "Three times has Henry Bolingbroke — King Henry IV — raised an army to fight against me and my army. Three times from the banks of the River Wye and the sandy-bottomed River Severn have I sent him home and weather-beaten back. It is bootless for him to try to fight me."

"Weather-beaten and bootless?" Hotspur said. "I wonder how the King managed to avoid catching a cold."

Glendower stopped arguing and said, "Here's the map. Let's look at it and make sure that we agree with the way that England has been divided into three parts: one-third for me, one-third for Mortimer, and one-third for Hotspur."

Mortimer said, "The Archdeacon of Bangor has divided it into three parts very equally. England, south and east from the River Trent and the River Severn, is my portion. Beyond the River Severn westward to Wales, and all the fertile land in that territory, goes to Owen Glendower. And, Hotspur, to you goes the territory north of the River Trent. Our three-part agreement has been drawn up. Let's review it and then have copies made so we can sign them tonight. Tomorrow, Hotspur, you and I and my good Lord of Worcester will set forth to meet your father and the Scottish army, as we agreed, at Shrewsbury. My father-in-law Glendower is not ready yet, but we will not need his help for fourteen days."

To Glendower, he said, "In that fourteen days, you will have time to assemble your army from the farmers working your land, your friends, and your neighboring allies."

"I intend to be ready sooner than that," Glendower said. "When I come to you, Hotspur and Mortimer, with my army, I will also bring your wives to you. Perhaps you should sneak away from them tonight without saying goodbye because they will shed a world of tears when you leave them."

Hotspur had been looking at the map; he was unhappy.

He said, "I think that my share of the land, north from the town of Burton here, in quantity equals not one of yours. You, Mortimer, and you, Glendower, have received more land than I have. See how this river comes winding into my territory and cuts from the best of all my land a huge half-Moon — a monstrous piece — out. I'll have the river dammed up here so that the smooth and silver River Trent shall run in a straight course in a new channel. It shall not wind with such a deep indent and rob me of so rich a valley here."

"You don't want the river to run there?" Glendower said. "It shall; it must; you can see that it does."

Mortimer said to Hotspur, "The river does flow into the valley but look here. It flows into a valley in my territory as much as it flows into the valley in your territory. It takes away from me and gives to you as much as it takes away from you and gives to me."

Worcester was not averse to Hotspur, his nephew, getting more land. He said, "With a little expense, we can move the river into a new course that will add some land to the north of the river and then the river will run straight and evenly."

"That's what I will do," Hotspur said. "It will cost only a little money."

Glendower, who wanted Mortimer, his son-in-law, to get all the land that was coming to him, said, "I will not allow the course of the river to be altered."

"Oh, won't you?" Hotspur said.

"No, I won't allow you to alter the course of the river."

"Who will stop me?"

"I will."

"I prefer not to understand you, so say it to me in Welsh," Hotspur said.

Glendower replied, "I can speak English, Hotspur, as well as you; for I was brought up in the English court, where, when I was young, I wrote song lyrics and set them to the music of the harp, thus giving the English beautiful poetry. This is something that I doubt that you have ever done."

You are right," Hotspur said, "and I am glad of it. I would prefer to be a kitten and cry 'meow' than to be one of these ballad-singers. I would prefer to hear the screech of a bronze candlestick being turned on a lathe that is normally used to make wooden candlesticks. I would prefer to hear a dry wheel grate and squeak on an axle. Would these things set my teeth on edge? Yes, but not as badly as would the sound of affected, high-falutin' poetry — it is like the hobbled gait of a shuffling nag."

Glendower gave in: "If you want to change the course of the River Trent, do so."

"No," Hotspur said. "I really don't care about the land. I'll give three times as much land to any well-deserving friend; but when it comes to making a bargain, understand me well, I'll argue about the ninth part of a hair."

He added, "Are the three copies of our agreement drawn up? Shall we sign them and leave?"

"The Moon shines brightly," Glendower said. "You may travel this night. I will go to the copyist and bid him to hurry. I will also tell your wives that you are leaving tonight. I am afraid my daughter will run mad because she loves her Mortimer so much."

Glendower departed.

Mortimer said, "Hotspur, you have a talent for making Glendower, my father-in-law, angry."

"I can't help it," Hotspur said. "Sometimes he makes me angry by telling me about a mole and an ant, about the magician Merlin and his prophecies, about a dragon and a finless fish, about a half-lion and half-eagle griffin with its wings clipped and a raven that has shed its feathers, about a lion resting on its legs and raising its head and a cat rearing up on its hind legs to attack. I think that the terms he used were a 'couching lion' and a 'ramping cat.' The Percy crest is the lion, the Glendower crest is the dragon, and the Mortimer crest is the wolf, and Glendower says that Henry IV is a mole and that the lion, the dragon, and the wolf will divvy up the mole's country. He says such things with such a massive amount of mumbo-jumbo and skimble-skamble stuff that he makes me lose my faith in him. I tell you, he bored me last night at least nine hours in reckoning up the names of the many Devils that are his lackeys. I said 'oh' and 'is that so?' but I did not listen to even a single word he said. Glendower is as tedious as a tired horse or a nagging wife. Glendower is worse than a smoky house. I would much prefer to live on cheese and garlic and live in a windmill than to eat delicacies and have him talk to me in any summer-house in the Christian part of the world."

Mortimer replied, "Actually, he is a worthy gentleman. He is very well read, and he is proficient in strange and occult arts. He is as valiant as a lion, and he is wondrously charming and as generous as the mines of India. Let me tell you that he holds you in high respect and he restrains his anger when you do or say something that makes him angry. I tell you that no other man could have done and said the things you do and say and not have been hurt in body or criticized with words. But avoid challenging him in the future, I beg you."

Worcester said to his nephew, "Truly, you are too hot-headed. Ever since you have come here, you have done and said many things to make Glendower angry. You need to learn to fix this fault of yours. Sometimes, plain-speaking can show greatness, courage, and spirit — and yes, you have those positive qualities — but sometimes, it serves only to antagonize others. Plain-speaking can show oneself to be full of harsh rage, to lack etiquette, to display loss of self-control, to be full of pride, haughtiness, and self-conceit, and to have a low opinion of other people. A nobleman who has any of these bad qualities will lose the friendship of other people. Possession of any of these bad qualities stains the person's good qualities and makes those good qualities difficult to be noticed and praised."

"Well, you have taught me well," Hotspur said. "May good manners bring you success."

Glendower entered the room, bringing with him the wives of Hotspur and Mortimer.

Hotspur said, "Here come our wives. Soon, we will leave them, so let's say our goodbyes."

Mortimer said, "What bothers me is that my wife can speak no English, and I can speak no Welsh."

His marriage to Glendower's daughter was a political marriage made to seal an alliance. Nevertheless, he and his wife of a short time were happily married.

Glendower said, "My daughter cries. She does not want to be parted from you. She wants to be a soldier and go with you to the war."

"Father-in-law, please tell her that she and Hotspur's wife will come with you when you join your army with our armies."

Glendower spoke to his daughter in Welsh, and she answered him in the same language.

Glendower said to Mortimer, "She is overly anxious to stay with you. She is being a silly girl and is unwilling to listen to reason."

Mortimer's wife spoke again, this time to him, in Welsh.

He said, "I understand your looks. Your pretty Welsh tears that pour down from your eyes I understand all too well. Except that I would be ashamed, I would communicate with you in the same way."

She kissed him and spoke again.

He said, "I understand your kisses and you understand mine. We are able to communicate our emotions. I will study hard and not be a truant until I have learned your language. Your voice makes Welsh as sweet as the most beautifully written lyrics sung by a beautiful Queen in a fine dwelling in summer to a tune played by a lute."

Glendower said to Mortimer, "Don't cry. You will only upset her."

Again, Mortimer's wife spoke to Mortimer in Welsh.

"Oh, I am completely ignorant when it comes to Welsh!" he said.

Glendower translated the content of what she had said: "She wants you to lie on the soft floor covering and to lay your head in her lap, and she will sing to you a song to please you and make you half-asleep and relaxed. You will be midway between waking and sleeping, just like twilight is midway between day and night during the hour before the Sun rises."

Mortimer replied, "With all my heart I will lie here and hear her sing. By the time she is finished, I think, the copies of our agreement will be completed."

"Enjoy," Glendower said. "Musicians shall play to you. Now they float in the air a thousand leagues from here, but immediately they shall arrive here. Lie down, and listen."

Hotspur said to Kate, his wife, "You are perfect at lying down."

She smiled, knowing the kind of lying down he meant.

Hotspur continued, "Sit down, so that I may rest my head in your lap."

"Stop it, you giddy goose," she said, aware that the words "head in your lap" have a sexual meaning, as well as an innocent meaning.

But she sat down and Hotspur non-sexually rested his head in her lap. He thought about Kate's threat to break his "little finger" earlier. "Little finger" did not necessarily have to mean a finger of his hand.

Music began to play, and Hotspur said, "Now I know that the Devil understands Welsh. Maybe that is why he is so moody. Still, he is a musician."

"In that case, you ought to be a good musician because you are so often moody," Kate said. "Lie still, you thief, and hear the lady sing in Welsh."

"I had rather hear Lady, my bitch-hound, howl in Irish."

"Do you want me to break your head?"

"No."

"Then be quiet."

"Never. That is a trait of women."

"God help you," Kate said.

Hotspur murmured, "To the Welsh lady's bed."

Not quite having heard his words, Kate asked, "What did you say?"

Hotspur replied, "Be quiet. She is singing."

Mortimer's wife sang a song in Welsh.

Hotspur said, "You shall sing a song next."

"No, I won't, for Heaven's sake."

"'For Heaven's sake!'" Hotspur said. "Kate, you are swearing like the wife of a candymaker. What will you say next: 'Darn it'? 'Gosh'? 'Golly'? Your swear words are like chiffon. It's like a preacher has raised you. Swear for me now, Kate, with blood and vigor. Swear the way the wife of Hotspur should swear. Fill your mouth with dirty words. Leave 'for Heaven's sake' and 'darn it' and such namby-pamby swearings to those who dress up on Sunday. Sing to me now a mouthful of words spiced with hot peppers."

"I will not sing," Kate said.

"Singing a normal song is a good way to become a tailor — tailors are known for singing as they work. It is also a good way to become a teacher of red-breasted songbirds," Hotspur said, and then he added, "I am going to go and see if the agreements have been copied. If they have been, I will be gone within two hours. Before I leave, come and see me."

He exited.

Glendower said to Mortimer, "Let's go now. You are as slow to leave here as Hotspur is on fire to go. By this time, our agreements will have been copied. We will sign them and affix our seals to them, and then we will mount our horses and leave."

Mortimer said, "I am ready."

They left to sign the copies of their agreement.

In a room in King Henry IV's palace in London, the King, Prince Hal, and others had been meeting.

King Henry IV said, "Everyone leave except for Prince Hal. The Prince of Wales and I must talk privately, but stay nearby because I shall need to talk to you again soon."

The others exited from the room.

The King said to Prince Hal, "I think that it is possible that God has secretly judged me because of some sin that I have committed and therefore is using you to punish and to torment me. The way that you are leading your life makes me think that your purpose in life is to give to me the hot vengeance of Heaven and to beat me with the rod of Heaven to punish me for my sins. Explain to me how else you could indulge in such unsuitable and low desires, such vulgar and despicable actions, and such barren pleasures, and how else could such vulgar friends become associated with you, who are the Prince of Wales?"

"Your majesty, my father," Prince Hal said, "I wish that I could clear myself of all the offenses charged against me as easily and clearly as I am certain that I can clear myself of many of these offenses charged against me. Yet let me ask of you one favor. The ears of great personages often hear false tales made up by smiling busybodies and gossips. If I can clear myself of many of these charges — and I can — I ask that I be forgiven for some youthful indiscretions, provided that I confess those indiscretions honestly."

"Let God forgive you!" the King said. "Harry, let me tell you that I am amazed at your personal desires, which are not those of your ancestors. Because of your violence, you have lost your place in council. John, your younger brother, now occupies that place. You are now almost absent from the hearts of all the members of my court and of your own relatives. The hopes and expectations that I had of your youth are ruined, and every man prophesies that you will fail. Had I acted the way that you are now acting — constantly appearing in public, showing myself often to the eyes of men who grow used to your presence, which is becoming stale and cheap to the common people — I would never have acquired the good opinion of the people. Instead, they would have stayed loyal to King Richard II, and I would still be in disgraceful banishment. I would not be King, and I would have no renown or success. I made sure that I was seldom seen in public, so that when I did appear in public I was to the common people like the rare sight of a comet. Men would tell their children, 'This is he.' Others would ask, 'Where? Which one is Bolingbroke?' I acted as graciously as an angel to the common people, and I acted with great humility. The result was that men pledged their allegiance to me with loud shouts and salutations from their mouths even when Richard was present. In that way, each appearance in public by me was fresh and new and to be wondered at. My presence was like a priest's ceremonial robe, seldom seen, and when seen, regarded with wonder. My appearances at occasions of state were seldom, but they were sumptuous like a feast. By being rarely seen, I inspired awe when I was seen.

"Richard II was my complete opposite. He was a flighty King, and he skipped and pranced and ambled and kept company with shallow jesters and rash wits who would flare up brightly but briefly and lacked lasting substance. He debased his royal self by mingling with capering fools, who profaned his name with crude jokes. He laughed at the jokes of boys and he allowed youths without beards to insult him, thus losing the majesty that belongs to a King. He became a frequent visitor to the common streets, and he attempted with his presence to make himself popular. Those who saw him soon became surfeited with the sight of him. He was like honey, which is good in small servings but when people have too much of it they begin to hate its sweetness, and even a little is too much. As King, he sometimes needed to present himself officially to the common people, but even at such solemn times, he was like the cuckoo in June — so common that no one bothers to look at it. They hear the cuckoo, but they ignore it. When people did look at Richard II, they did not look at him as if he were special — they had seen him too often to regard seeing him as anything special. But when a King is seldom seen, then people look at him with an extraordinary gaze — that is what happens when Sun-like majesty shines seldom in admiring eyes. But when Richard showed himself, the common people dozed and their eyelids drooped. They slept right in front of him, not showing him respect, and when they did wake up and look at him it was with such a look as sullen men give to their enemies. He had appeared before them so often that they were glutted, gorged, and full with his presence.

"You, Harry, are now just like he was then. You have lost the respect that should be given to a Prince. Why? Because you associate with base low-lives. Everyone's eyes are weary of seeing you because they see you so often, except for my eyes, which would like to see you more often. And now my eyes are doing that which I do not want them to do, blinding me with tears of foolish tenderness."

Prince Hal promised, "From now on, my very gracious father, I will act more like myself — more like a Prince ought to act."

King Henry IV said, "For all the world, you are now as King Richard II was then. As I was when I traveled out of my exile in France and set foot at Ravenspurgh, so is Hotspur now. I swear by my scepter and by my soul that he has a better claim than you to the throne. His claim to the throne rests on accomplishments; your claim to the throne is a mere matter of birth. Hotspur has no hereditary right to the throne or anything even resembling a hereditary right to the throne, and yet he has filled battlefields with men in armor and he is at the head of an army that is opposed to me, the King. Even though he is the same young age as you, he leads old lords and reverend bishops on to bloody battles and to violent war. Hotspur earned never-dying honor by fighting against the renowned Douglas! Hotspur's high deeds, hot incursions, and great name in arms have given him a reputation as the supreme and preeminent soldier throughout all of the Christian nations. Three times has the young Hotspur, a Mars in swaddling clothes, an infant warrior, in battles defeated great Douglas. He has captured him once, freed him, and made a friend of him so that Douglas would join the rebellion and shake the peace and security of our throne.

"What have you to say to this? Percy, Northumberland, the Archbishop of York, Douglas, and Mortimer all are rebelling against us and are up in arms. But why am I telling you this? Why, Harry, do I tell you about my foes, when you are my nearest and dearest enemy? You, Harry, are very likely, through being a slave to fear, base inclination, and ill temper, to fight against me. You would accept the pay of a mercenary from Hotspur, you would follow at his heels like a dog, and you would bow to him when he frowns at you. You would do all of these things in order to hurt me by showing me how degenerate you are."

Prince Hal replied, "Do not think that. It is not true. God forgive those who have so much swayed your majesty's good thoughts away from me! I will redeem all this on Hotspur's head during battle. At sunset of some glorious day, I will be so bold as to tell you that I am your son. On that day, I will wear a garment all covered with blood and my face will be encased in a mask made of blood. This blood, when washed away, shall wash away my shame with it. All of this will happen, I swear, on the day, whenever it occurs, that this child of honor and renown, this gallant Hotspur, this all-praised knight, and your own Harry with the bad reputation shall happen to meet in battle. I wish that Hotspur's honors and glories were multiplied many times and that my shames and indignities were doubled because when he and I meet in battle, I shall make this northern youth — this Hotspur — exchange his honors and glories for my shames and indignities. Hotspur, although he does not know it, will be the means of my redemption. He has accomplished many glorious deeds, but in battle I shall make him give up every glorious deed and every honor, no matter how small. By defeating Hotspur, I shall win for myself greater glory and honor than he has accrued. I swear to God that this shall be so. I shall tear Hotspur's glory and honor from his heart. I pray that God allows this to happen. If He allows it, I beg that your majesty may forgive the long-grown wounds of my intemperate behavior. If God does not allow this to happen, then I will die on the battlefield and my death will cancel all the debts I owe to the living. I swear that I will die a hundred thousand deaths on the battlefield before I break even the smallest part of my vow."

King Henry IV said, "As a result of your vow, a hundred thousand rebels will die! You will have command of troops and my complete trust."

Sir Walter Blunt entered the room.

"How are you, Sir Walter?" King Henry IV asked. "You look serious."

"The news that I have come to tell you is serious," Blunt said. "A Scottish nobleman has sent word that Douglas and the English rebels have joined forces the eleventh of this month at Shrewsbury. If all the rebels keep their promises and show up with their armies, they will have as mighty and fearsome a force as has ever committed foul play in England."

"Our armies are also setting forth," King Henry IV said. "The Earl of Westmoreland and an army set forth today; with him went my son, Lord John of Lancaster. For five days, I have known about the news you bring. This coming Wednesday, Harry, you shall set forth with an army. On Thursday, I will set forth with an army and go to Bridgenorth. Harry, you will march through

Gloucestershire. In twelve days, all of our armies will meet at Bridgenorth. We have much to do. Let's get to work. People who delay grow fat and tired."

At the Boar's-Head Tavern in Eastcheap, Bardolph and Falstaff were talking.

Falstaff said, "Bardolph, have I not lost weight since the robbery at Gadshill? Does not my weight decline? Do I not dwindle? Why, my skin hangs about me like an old lady's loose gown. I am withered like a shriveled old apple. Well, I'll repent, and that at once, now that I am in the mood and something still remains of my body. Soon, I will be in a different mood and bodily condition, and then I won't have the strength to repent. If I have not forgotten what the inside of a church looks like, I am withered like a peppercorn or a decrepit horse that belongs to a brewer. Company, villainous company, has been the ruin of me."

Bardolph said, "Sir John, you are so fretful and complain so much that you cannot live long."

"You're right," Falstaff said. "Sing a bawdy song to me to make me merry. I have lived as virtuously as a gentleman needs to be. I have been virtuous enough. I have sworn only a little; gambled not ... more than seven times a week; went to a bawdy-house not more than once ... in a quarter of an hour; paid back money that I borrowed ... three or four times; lived well and in good compass. Now I live out of all order, out of all compass."

"Why, you are so fat, Sir John, that you must be out of all compass, out of all reasonable compass, Sir John," Bardolph said. "Your girth vastly exceeds the average, so any belt that encompasses your belly will greatly exceed the average."

Falstaff, who was not pleased to hear this, said to the fiery-faced Bardolph, "Fix your face, and I will fix my life. You are a flagship, as we can tell by the lantern, but a flagship has its lantern in the rear, and you bear a lantern in your nose. You are the Knight of the Burning Lamp."

"Why, Sir John, my face does you no harm."

"You are right, of course," Falstaff said. "In fact, I make good use of your face. Many men have rings that are engraved with a Death's-head, and many men keep skulls as a *memento mori* — a reminder of death — for all of us shall die some day. I never see your face but that I think about hell-fire and Dives, the rich man who wore purple; for there he is in his robes, burning, burning. If you were in any way virtuous, I would swear by your face. My oath would be

'By this fire that is God's angel' because of all the accounts in the Bible of angels manifesting themselves as fire. Unfortunately, you are altogether given over to evil, and you would be, if not for the light in your face, the son of utter darkness. After the robbery, you ran up Gadshill at night to catch my horse, and I'll be damned if I didn't think you were an *ignis fatuus* or fireworks. If that isn't true, then money won't buy anything. Oh, you are a perpetual torch-lit procession, an everlasting bonfire-light! You have saved me a thousand marks in lamps and torches as I have walked with you in the night between tavern and tavern; however, the money for sack that you have drunk would have bought me much light at the shop of the most expensive candlemaker in Europe. Salamanders are thought to live in fire. I have maintained that salamander nose of yours with fire — and you with sack to make your nose red — for the past two and thirty years. May God reward me for it!"

Bardolph replied, "I wish that my face were in your belly!"

"Then God have mercy on me," Falstaff said, "because I would be sure to suffer from heartburn."

The Hostess entered the room.

"Hello, Dame Partlet the hen!" Falstaff said. "Have you inquired yet who picked my pockets?"

The Hostess, who was upset at the accusation of Falstaff's pockets being picked in her inn, said, "Why, Sir John, what do you think, Sir John? Do you think I keep thieves in my house? I have searched, I have inquired, and so has my husband, man by man, boy by boy, servant by servant. The tenth part of a hair was never lost in my inn before."

Falstaff replied, "You lie, Hostess. Bardolph was shaved and lost many a hair here, and I swear that my pockets were picked. You are a woman, so you know about deceit."

The Hostess, who knew that Falstaff was capable of making witty insults and so was on guard against being insulted, replied, "Who is a woman? Am I? No! I deny what you said! By God, I was never called that in my own inn before."

"Go on, I know you well enough," Falstaff said.

The Hostess replied, "No, Sir John, you do not know me, Sir John. I know you, Sir John. You owe me money, Sir John, and now you pick a quarrel to beguile me of it. I bought you a dozen shirts to wear."

"They were made of dowlas, filthy dowlas — cheap linen. I gave them to bakers' wives to make sieves out of them."

"As I am a true woman," the Hostess said, "they were made out of fine linen — holland that cost eight shillings an ell. You also owe money here, Sir John, for your meals and for your drinks, and for money lent to you — four and twenty pounds."

Falstaff pointed at Bardolph and said, "He had his part of it; let him pay."

"He?" the Hostess said, "He is poor; he has nothing."

"Poor?" Falstaff said. "Look at the red-gold and copper tones of his face. If he turns the red-gold and copper into coins, he will be rich. As for me, I will not pay the tenth part of a penny. Are you trying to treat me like an ignorant youngster? Can't I even relax in an inn without having my pockets picked? I have lost a seal-ring of my grandfather's that is worth forty marks."

"I have heard the Prince say many times that your ring is only copper."

"Ha!" Falstaff said. "Prince Hal is a rascal. He is a sneak. If he were here, I would beat him like a dog if he were to say that my ring is made of copper." He grabbed a walking stick and demonstrated.

This speech was badly timed because Prince Hal and Peto entered the room, marching as if going to war. Falstaff pretended that the walking stick was a flute and he accompanied the marchers.

Falstaff said, "What is the news? By your actions, I can guess that we must all march off to war."

"Yes, we must march," Bardolph said. "We will march two by two in pairs like prisoners being taken to Newgate Prison."

The Hostess said to Prince Hal, "My lord, please hear what I have to say."

"What do you have to say, Mistress Quickly?" Prince Hal replied. "How is your husband? I much respect him, for he is an honest man."

The Hostess repeated, "My good lord, listen to me."

Falstaff knew what she wanted to say, and so he said to Prince Hal, "Ignore her, and listen to me."

"What have you got to say, Jack?" Prince Hal said to Falstaff.

Falstaff said, "The other night I fell asleep here in the alcove behind the wall hanging and someone picked my pockets. This inn has apparently been turned into a bawdy-house; people pick pockets in whorehouses."

Prince Hal, who knew exactly what Falstaff had had in his pockets, asked, "What did you lose, Jack?"

"Would you believe it, Hal," Falstaff replied, "I lost three or four IOUs each worth forty pounds, and I lost a seal-ring that had belonged to my grandfather."

"The ring was a trifle, worth around eight pennies," Prince Hal said.

"That's what I told him," the Hostess said. "I said that I had heard you say so, and, my lord, he speaks most vilely of you, like the foul-mouthed man he is — he said that he would beat you with a stick."

"What!" Prince Hal said. "Did he really say that?"

The Hostess replied, "There's neither faith, truth, nor womanhood in me else."

Falstaff, who did not want to get in trouble with the Prince, said to her, "There's no more faith in you than in a stewed prune served in a whorehouse, or more accurately, there's no more faith in you than in a whore. There is no more truth in you than in a fox that is willing to play every trick on hunters that it knows in order to get back safe and sound to its lair. As for womanhood, the wanton maid known as Marian is like the virtuous wife of an officer of the law or a preacher in comparison to you. Go away, you thing."

"Thing?" the Hostess cried. "What kind of thing do you think I am?"

"What thing! Why, a thing to thank God for."

Afraid that she had been insulted, the Hostess said, "I am no thing to thank God for — I wish you knew that! I am an honest man's wife, and, even though you are a Knight, you are a knave to call me so."

"Even though you are a woman, you are a beast to say that," Falstaff said.

"What kind of beast am I, knave?" the Hostess asked.

"What kind of beast! Why, you are an otter."

Surprised by the answer, Prince Hal asked, "An otter, Sir John? Why an otter?"

"Why, she's neither fish nor flesh; a man knows not where to have her."

Afraid once more that she had been insulted, the Hostess said, "You are wrong when you say that. You or any man knows where to have me, you knave, you!"

The Prince knew the sexual meaning of having a woman; he smiled and said, "Hostess, you say the truth, and Falstaff has slandered you most grossly."

"He has lied about you, too," the Hostess replied. "Just the other day he said that you owed him a thousand pounds."

Prince Hal said to Falstaff, "Creep, do I owe you a thousand pounds?"

Quick-thinking Falstaff replied, "A thousand pounds, Hal? You owe me a million pounds. Your love is worth a million pounds, and you owe me your love."

The Hostess said, "My lord, he called you a rascal, and he said he would beat you."

Falstaff asked, "Did I, Bardolph?"

Falstaff expected Bardolph to back him up and say that he had not threatened to beat the Prince, but Bardolph was still sore about the comments that Falstaff had made about his face and replied, "Indeed, Sir John, you said so."

"Yes, if he said my ring was copper," Falstaff said.

"I do say that it is made of copper," Prince Hal said. "Do you dare to be as good as your word now?"

"Why, Hal, you know, as you are a man, I dare. However, you are a Prince, and I fear you as a Prince as I fear the roaring of a lion's pup."

"And why not as the lion?"

"The King is to be feared as the lion. Do you think that I would fear you as I fear your father? No, and if I do, I pray to God that my belt will break."

"If it does, your guts will fall down to your knees," Prince Hal said. "But there's no room for faith, truth, or honesty in your bosom — it is all filled up with guts and belly fat. Accuse an honest woman of picking your pockets! Why, you son of a whore, you impudent, swollen-up rascal, if there were anything in your pockets but tavern-reckonings, keepsakes from bawdy-houses, and one poor penny's worth of sugar-candy to make you long-winded, if your pockets were enriched with anything but these, I am a villain. Yet you continue to pretend that you have been robbed of valuables and you will not admit that you are wrong. Aren't you ashamed?"

"But, Hal, Adam fell in the days of innocence in the Garden of Eden, so what can you expect of poor Jack Falstaff in these days of villany? You can see that I have more flesh than another man, and therefore I have more frailty. You confess then that you picked my pockets?"

"It appears so by my story."

Falstaff exclaimed, "Hostess, I forgive you. Go and make my breakfast. Love your husband, tend to your servants, and cherish your guests. You shall find me reasonable. As you can see, I am calm and peaceful again. Go now."

Happy to be forgiven, the Hostess departed to make Falstaff's breakfast.

Falstaff turned to Prince Hal and asked, "What news do you have? What about the robbery?"

"Oh, my sweet beef," Prince Hal said, "I am still your guardian angel. The money you robbed has been paid back."

Falstaff said, "I do not like that paying back; it is a double labor. First comes the stealing, and then comes the paying back."

Prince Hal said, "My other news is that I am again on good terms with my father. He trusts me again."

"Use that trust to rob the treasury for me," Falstaff said. "And don't bother to stop and wash your hands before you commit the robbery."

"Please do what Falstaff said," Bardolph said.

Prince Hal said, "I have procured for you, Jack, a charge of ... foot."

"I wish it were a charge of cavalry," Falstaff said. "Where shall I find a competent thief to steal a horse for me? I need a fine thief of the age of two and twenty or thereabouts! I am dreadfully unequipped. Well, God be thanked for these rebels — they offend none but the virtuous. The unvirtuous can always find a way to turn a war to their advantage. I laud the rebels — I praise them."

"Bardolph," Prince Hal said.

"Yes, my lord?"

"Go and deliver this letter to Lord John of Lancaster, my brother. Go and deliver this letter to my Lord of Westmoreland."

Bardolph departed to do his errands.

"Peto, get our horses ready," Prince Hal said. "You and I have thirty miles to ride before dinnertime."

Peto departed to do his errand.

To Falstaff, Prince Hal said, "Jack, meet me tomorrow in the temple hall at two o'clock in the afternoon. There you shall get your orders as well as money to pay for your troops' equipment."

Prince Hal added, "The land is burning; Hotspur stands on high; and either we or they must lower lie. Many men will soon lower lie in their graves."

Prince Hal departed.

To himself, Falstaff said, "Those are well-spoken words, and this is a splendid world. I can find ways to profit from war."

He called, "Hostess, bring me my breakfast!"

Then he said to himself, "I wish I could stay in this tavern and make a profit while other people fight in the war."

CHAPTER 4

— 4.1 —

Hotspur, Worcester, and Douglas were meeting in the rebel camp near Shrewsbury. Hotspur and Douglas, recently become allies, were complimenting each other. Hotspur was taking the advice of Worcester to be more diplomatic.

Hotspur replied to something that the Earl of Douglas, whom Hotspur had defeated in battle three times, had said, "Well said, my noble Scot. If speaking the truth in this fine age were not thought to be flattery, such praise would you, the Earl of Douglas, have that no one who became a soldier in this campaign would have so good a reputation as yours throughout the world. By God, I am incapable of flattery; I hate the tongues of flatterers; but no man has a better place in my heart than you do. If you should ever test my friendship for you, my friendship would prove to be true."

Douglas replied, "You are the King of Honor. If any man states that you are not, I will fight him."

"You would do that," Hotspur said. "Well said."

A messenger arrived, carrying letters.

Hotspur said, "What letters do you have there?"

The messenger gave Hotspur the letters, and Hotspur said, "Thank you."

The messenger said, "These letters come from your father, Northumberland."

"Letters from him!" Hotspur said. "Why hasn't he come here in person?"

"He cannot come, my lord. He is grievously ill."

"Damn!" Hotspur said. "How can he have the leisure to be sick in such an exciting and turbulent time? Who leads his army? Who is their general?"

"His letters should tell you that," the messenger said. "I cannot, my lord."

Worcester asked, "Is he bedridden?"

"He was unable to get out of bed for the four days before I set forth. At the time of my departure from his castle, his physicians feared that he might die."

"I wish that this rebellion had been finished before he got sick," Worcester said. "We have never needed him to be in good health more than now."

Hotspur read the letters.

"Sick now! Droop now!" Hotspur said. "His sickness infects the very life-blood of our rebellion. His sickness spreads even to our rebel camp. He writes me here that he has some internal sickness ... and that his allies could not be assembled in time by anyone he could delegate. Also, he did not think it wise to allow anyone other than himself to perform so dangerous and important a task. But he also advises us to boldly continue with our small army and fight and see if we win because, he writes, we can't draw back now because King Henry IV is certainly aware of our rebellion. What do you think of this information?"

Worcester said, "Your father's sickness deeply hurts us. It is a maim to our rebellion."

Hotspur replied, "It is a perilous gash! It is a limb cut off!"

He paused, and then he said, "And yet, I believe, it is not. The absence of my father and his army seems more serious than we shall find it. Is it wise to stake all of our resources on one battle? Should we bet everything on one throw of the dice? Should everything be risked in one hazardous action when such a rich prize is at stake? No. If we were to risk everything we had, that would mean that we had reached the very end of our hopes and the very limits of our resources."

"You are right," Douglas said. "We have forces in reserve. It is as if we are expecting an inheritance. We can boldly spend what we have now, knowing that soon we will have more. We have something to fall back on; that is our comfort."

Hotspur said, "We have a place to go to. We have a refuge in case the Devil and mischance bring us early defeat in our rebellion."

"Still, I wish that your father were here," Worcester said. "We must be united in our rebellion. Some people who do not know the reason for your father's absence may think that his knowledge and wisdom, loyalty to King Henry IV, and dislike of our rebellion has kept him from joining forces with us. Think how such a perception may affect our more timid supporters and make them wonder about the justness of our cause. We who take the offensive in a rebellion must avoid careful evaluations of our cause. We must make sure the eyes of those who would find fault in our rebellion see nothing. Your father's absence opens a curtain through which our supporters may find reasons to become frightened and not support us."

"You worry too much," Hotspur said. "We can look at my father's absence as being an advantage. It gives our rebellion a brighter and greater renown because our rebellion is now more daring because my father and his army are not here. People will think that if we can raise an army to challenge the King without my father's help, then once my father's army joins us, we shall topple Henry IV's kingdom and depose him. All is still well; our rebellion is still sound."

"That's true," Douglas said. "In Scotland we don't know the meaning of the word 'fear.'"

Sir Richard Vernon walked over to the three leaders of the rebellion.

"Welcome, Vernon," Hotspur said.

"I hope that my news will be welcome," Vernon said. "The Earl of Westmoreland, with an army seven thousand strong, is marching here. With him is Prince John."

"No problem," Hotspur said. "What other news do you bring?"

"In addition, I have learned that King Henry IV himself in person has either already set forth or will set forth soon and will arrive here with a strong and mighty army."

"That is also not a problem," Hotspur said. "Where are his son, the nimble-footed and zany Prince of Wales, and the Prince's friends, all of whom prefer drinking to anything else in the world?"

"I can report that Prince Hal is with an army, all well-equipped and well-armed. His soldiers are all plumed with ostrich feathers — the emblem of the Prince of Wales — shaking their wings like eagles after a bath, glittering in golden coats of armor like statues, as full of spirit as the month of May, and as gorgeous as the midsummer Sun, as sportive as young goats, and as wild as young bulls. I myself saw young Prince Hal, with his helmet on, his thighs covered with armor, and gallantly furnished with weapons, rise from the ground like the messenger god Mercury with feathered ankles that make him fast. Prince Hal vaulted with such ease into his saddle as if an angel had dropped down from the clouds to ride a fiery Pegasus and bewitch the world with his noble horsemanship."

"Stop! Stop!" Hotspur said. "This praise is making me sick — it's like catching a cold with a change of season. Let them come. They come like beasts for sacrifice in their fine armor. All hot and bleeding we will offer them to Bellona, the fire-eyed maiden of smoky war. The god of war, Mars, shall sit on his altar up to his ears in blood. I am on fire, knowing that this rich prize is so near and is not yet ours. Come, let me mount my horse and feel him underneath me. My horse will carry me like a thunderbolt against the Prince of Wales. Harry Hotspur and Prince Harry shall meet — on one hot horse against another hot horse — and never part until one of us is made a corpse."

Hotspur paused and then said, "I wish that Glendower were here with his army!"

Vernon said, "I have more bad news. I learned in the city of Worcester, as I rode along, that Glendower was not able to assemble his army."

Douglas said, "That is the worst news that I have heard yet."

"Yes," Worcester said. "This is chilling news."

Hotspur asked, "How many soldiers does King Henry IV have."

"Approximately thirty thousand."

"Let it be forty thousand," Hotspur said. "My father and Glendower and their armies are not here, but our armies may still bring us victory. Let's quickly gather our troops. Doomsday is near. If we all will die, let us die merrily."

"Don't talk about dying," Douglas said. "I refuse to be afraid of dying for the next six months. Talk of dying is bad for morale."

Falstaff and Bardolph were talking in a public road near Coventry. Falstaff's company of men whom he had drafted into military service for King Henry IV were with them.

Falstaff said, "Bardolph, go before me to Coventry. Fill up a bottle of sack for me. Our soldiers shall continue to march. Tonight we will reach Sutton Coldfill."

"Will you give me money to pay for the sack, Captain?" Bardolph asked.

"Use your own money," Falstaff replied.

"'This bottle will make your debt ten shillings," Bardolph calculated. "Ten shillings equal an angel, so this bottle will make one angel."

Falstaff pretended that the bottle could actually make angels: "If it makes an angel, keep it in return for your labor. If it makes twenty angels, keep them all. Since they are angels, I am sure that the coinage is good. Tell Lieutenant Peto to meet me at the edge of the town."

"I will, Captain," Bardolph said. "Goodbye."

He departed.

Falstaff said to himself, "If I am not ashamed of my soldiers, I am a pickled fish. I have damnably misused the King's power of drafting citizens to fight in the war. I drafted a hundred and fifty people, but for three hundred and odd pounds, they bribed me to draft other people to be soldiers. I was able to get all this money by drafting no one except people with money. I drafted wealthy property-owners and the sons of wealthy farmers. I inquired about men who were about to be married and drafted them. I drafted people who live comfortably and who would rather hear the Devil than to hear the sound of a military drum. I drafted wealthy people who love comfort and are more afraid of the sound of a gun than is a wild duck that has been shot. I drafted only weaklings who dine on toast and butter, who have hearts no bigger than the heads of pins. All of these people have paid me not to draft them, and now my company officially consists of lots of ensigns, corporals, lieutenants, and other junior officers. The rich people I drafted I made officers; that entitled them to more pay. The rich people paid me to draft someone else, and I then drafted privates, who don't make much money, and now I keep for myself the difference in pay.

"My company consists of rascals as ragged as Lazarus in scenes on a painted cloth where the glutton's dogs licked Lazarus' sores. These people now in my company were never soldiers: They are servants who were fired because they were dishonest; they are the younger sons of younger brothers, and so they are impoverished; they are apprentice bartenders who ran away from their servitude; and they are unemployed hostlers. They are parasites even when the world is calm and has been long at peace. They are ten times more dishonorably ragged than is an old tattered flag. Such are the kinds of men whom I have drafted to fight in the King's war. Anyone who would look at them would think that I had a hundred and fifty tattered prodigal sons recently come from keeping swine and from eating hog swill and garbage. A madcap fellow met me on the road, looked at my men, and told me that I had unloaded all the gibbets and drafted the dead bodies.

"No eye has ever seen such scarecrows. I'll not march through Coventry with them — that's for certain. Coventry has a prison, and my 'soldiers' might be arrested as suspected escaped prisoners because my 'soldiers' march with a wide space between their legs, as if they had fetters on their legs; and indeed I got most of them out of prison — prisoners are sometimes released so they can fight in a war.

"There's but a shirt and a half in my entire company. The half-shirt is two handkerchiefs attached together and thrown over the shoulders like the sleeveless coat of a herald. The whole shirt, to say the truth, was stolen from my host at Saint Albans, or from the red-nosed innkeeper at Daventry. But that doesn't matter. The members of my company can steal shirts that are set out on hedges to dry after being washed."

Prince Hal and the Lord of Westmoreland rode up to Falstaff and his company.

"How are you, fat Jack! How are you, thickly quilted friend!" Prince Hal said.

"What, Hal! How are you, mad wag!" Falstaff replied. "What the Devil are you doing in Warwickshire?"

He noticed Westmoreland and said, "My good Lord of Westmoreland, pardon me for not greeting you more quickly. I thought that you had already reached Shrewsbury."

"To be honest," Westmoreland said, "I ought to be there already, and so should you. But my soldiers are already there. The King, I can tell you, is looking for all of us. We must march all night."

"Don't worry about me," Falstaff said. "I am as vigilant as a cat on the lookout to steal cream."

"I think that you have already stolen the cream and drunk it, too," Prince Hal said. "It has been churned in your belly and turned into butter. But tell me, Jack, whose fellows are these behind you?"

"Mine, Hal," Falstaff said. "They are mine."

"I never did see such pitiful rascals."

"Tut, tut," Falstaff said. "These men are good enough to be stabbed by a bayonet and then tossed aside. They are good enough to be food for gunpowder. They will fill a pit of corpses as well as better men. They are mortal men after all."

The purpose of war is to kill men, Falstaff thought. *Why kill the best men? Why not kill the worst men? Why not kill the men who are not valued?*

"True," Westmoreland said, "but, Sir John, I think that they are exceedingly poor and bare-bone — exceedingly beggarly."

Westmoreland thought, *These men are inferior and threadbare.*

"They know poverty," Falstaff said, "but I do not know how they came to learn that. These men are lean, certainly, but they did not learn that from me."

"No," Prince Hal said. "They did not learn leanness from you, unless you call three fingers of fat over the ribs lean. But hurry to Shrewsbury. Hotspur is already camped near there."

"Is the King there, too?" Falstaff asked.

"He is, Sir John," Westmoreland said. "I fear we shall stay behind too long and miss the battle."

Prince Hal and Westmoreland departed.

Falstaff said to himself, "I am a dull and sluggish fighter and so I don't mind showing up at the end of a battle; however, I am a keen and hungry guest and so I always show up at the beginning of a feast."

— 4.3 —

Hotspur, the Earl of Worcester, the Earl of Douglas, and Sir Richard Vernon debated battle tactics in the rebel camp near Shrewsbury.

"Let's fight tonight," Hotspur said.

"No," Worcester said. "That's a bad idea."

Douglas said, "If we do not fight this night, then we give the King the advantage."

"That is not true," Sir Richard Vernon said.

"Why do you say that?" Hotspur asked. "Isn't the King looking for reinforcements?"

"So are we."

"The King's reinforcements are sure to arrive," Hotspur said. "Our reinforcements may or may not arrive."

"Hotspur, take my advice," Worcester said. "Let's not fight the King tonight."

"I agree," Sir Richard Vernon said. "Let's not fight tonight."

"This is poor advice," Douglas said. "It is based on fear and cowardice."

"Don't slander me, Douglas," Sir Richard Vernon said. "I swear on my life, and I will back up what I say with my life, that although I fight after carefully considering what is the best thing to do, I fight with as little fear as you or as any Scot who lives today. Tomorrow we will see which of us is afraid in the battle."

"Or we will find out tonight," Douglas said.

"At either time, I will show no fear," Sir Richard Vernon said.

"I say that we shall fight tonight," Hotspur said.

"Tonight is a bad time for fighting," Sir Richard Vernon said. "You, Hotspur, and you, Douglas, are great leaders, and you should be able to see the reasons why we should not fight tonight. We face many problems. Some cavalry led by my kinsman have not arrived. Your uncle Worcester's cavalry arrived only today, and now their spirit is asleep and their courage is tame and dull because of exhaustion from hard labor. Not a horse is half the half of himself."

"The same thing is true of the horses in the King's cavalry," Hotspur said. "In general, the King's horses are weary and brought low from travel. The majority of our horses are rested."

"The number of the King's horses is greater than ours," Worcester said. "For God's sake, Hotspur, let's wait until all our cavalry have arrived."

A trumpet sounded to announce a visitor from King Henry IV, and Sir Walter Blunt walked into the rebel camp.

He said, "I come with gracious offers from the King, if you will listen to them."

"Welcome, Sir Walter Blunt," Hotspur said with respect. "I wish to God that you were on our side! Some of us respect you very well, but we begrudge you your great honor and good name because you are fighting not on our side but for our enemy."

"God forbid that I should be on your side as long as you step outside the bounds of decency and oppose your legitimate and anointed majesty," Sir Walter Blunt replied. "But let me convey to you my message from the King. He wants to know the nature of your grievances and why in this time of civil peace you are stirring up war and spreading bold hostility, dissent, and rebellion throughout his loyal land. If the King has in any way forgotten your good actions, which he admits are many, he asks you to list your complaints, and he will as quickly as possible meet your demands — with interest. He will also give an absolute pardon to you and to your troops whom you have misled."

Hotspur replied, "The King is kind, and we know well that the King knows when to promise and when to pay. My father and my uncle and myself did give him that same royalty he wears. We are the ones who made him King. When he had not even twenty-six soldiers supporting him, when the world had a low opinion of him, when he was wretched and low, a poor and forsaken outlaw sneaking home, my father gave him welcome to the shore of England. And when my father heard Henry Bolingbroke swear and vow to God that he had returned to England only to gain his rightful title of Duke of Lancaster, to sue for the return of his lands, and to make peace with King Richard II with tears of innocence and declarations of loyalty, my father, because of his kind heart and because he was moved by pity, swore to help him and delivered that help that he had promised.

"When the lords and barons of the realm perceived that my father, the Earl of Northumberland, supported Henry Bolingbroke, both the higher and the lower classes came and showed their allegiance to him by taking off their caps and bending their knees. They met him in boroughs, cities, and villages, waited for him on bridges, stood in rows and let him pass between them, laid gifts before him, gave him their oaths to support him, gave him their heirs to serve him as pages, and followed at his heels in celebration.

"Henry Bolingbroke presently understood his new power, and he became more ambitious than he was in the vow he made to my father upon the shore at Ravenspurgh when he, Henry Bolingbroke, was still humble and had little power. He then took on himself to reform certain laws and strict decrees that weighed too heavily on the country. He cried out against abuses, and he pretended to weep over wrongs that hurt England. With this image, this mask that pretended justice, he won the hearts of all whom he wanted to back him. He then proceeded further and cut off the heads of all the deputies whom the absent King Richard II had left behind here in England while he was personally fighting in the war in Ireland."

"I did not come here to hear this," Sir Walter Blunt said.

"Allow me to get to the point," Hotspur said. "Shortly afterward, Henry Bolingbroke deposed King Richard II. Soon after that, he took away the King's life. Following that, he taxed the entire country. Even worse, he then allowed Mortimer to be held as hostage in Wales, and he refused to ransom him. If Mortimer now held the office that he by rights ought to have, he would be King instead of Henry Bolingbroke. King Henry IV also disgraced me despite my many military victories, sent spies to gather information to be used against me, berated my uncle Worcester and drove him away from the council board, and in rage dismissed my father from the court. He has broken oath on oath and committed wrong on wrong. In conclusion, he has driven us to raise an army to protect ourselves and to question his title to the crown. Henry Bolingbroke is not in the direct line of descent from Richard II, and so we think that his claim to be King is weak and ought not to be endured."

Sir Walter Blunt asked, "Shall I return this answer to the King?"

"No," Hotspur said. "We will think over our final answer tonight. Go now to King Henry IV, and ask him to send us a hostage to ensure the safe return of my uncle Worcester, who will go to the King tomorrow morning and tell him our demands."

"I wish that you would accept the King's offer of kindness and respect," Sir Walter Blunt said.

"Perhaps we will," Hotspur replied.

"I pray God that you do," Sir Walter Blunt said.

In his palace, the Archbishop of York talked to Sir Michael.

The Archbishop of York said, "Sir Michael, take this sealed message quickly to the lord marshal, this message to my kinsman Scroop, and all the other messages to those to whom they are addressed. If you knew how important these messages are, you would be vigilant and deliver them very quickly."

"My good lord, I can guess what their content is."

"I think you can," the Archbishop of York said. "Tomorrow, Sir Michael, is a day during which ten thousand men will be tested. At Shrewsbury, I understand that the King with a mighty and quickly raised army will fight against Hotspur's army. Sir Michael, because of the illness of Northumberland, whose army would be huge had he been healthy enough to raise it, and because of the absence of the army of Owen Glendower, who was counted on to provide needed strength but has stayed away because of prophecies, I am afraid that the army of Hotspur is too weak to risk a battle with the King's army."

"Why, my good lord, you need not fear," Sir Michael said. "Hotspur will be aided by Douglas and Lord Mortimer."

"No, Mortimer is not there."

"But there is Mordake, Sir Richard Vernon, Hotspur, the Earl of Worcester, and many other gallant warriors and noble gentlemen."

"That's true," the Archbishop of York said, "but the King has gathered the best men of all the land to fight for him: the Prince of Wales, Lord John of Lancaster, the noble Westmoreland, and warlike Sir Walter Blunt; in addition, the King has gathered many other associates and respected men who are skilled in the arts of war."

"You can be sure, my lord, that they shall be well opposed."

"I hope so," the Archbishop of York said, "yet I have reason to fear Hotspur's defeat in battle. And so, to prevent the worst that can happen, Sir Michael, hurry and deliver these letters. If Hotspur is defeated in battle, King Henry IV will attack us next because he has learned of our part in the rebellion, and it is wise for us to prepare to oppose him as strongly as we can. Therefore ,make haste. I must write to other friends, and so, farewell, Sir Michael."

CHAPTER 5

— 5.1 —

The next morning, on 21 July 1403, King Henry IV, Prince Hal, Lord John of Lancaster, Sir Walter Blunt, and Falstaff met in the King's camp near Shrewsbury

King Henry IV said, "The Sun is red like blood as it begins to appear over that bushy mountain. It seems ill and feverish, and the day is pale in comparison."

Prince Hal said, "The southern wind blows as if it is playing a trumpet and announcing what the Sun means by its appearance. The hollow whistling in the leaves foretells a stormy and windy day."

"Let the weather sympathize with the losers of the upcoming battle," King Henry IV said. "Nothing can seem foul to those who win."

A trumpet sounded.

The Earl of Worcester and Sir Richard Vernon came into the King's camp.

The King said, "How are you, my Lord of Worcester! It is not good that you and I should meet upon such terms as now we meet. You have deceived our trust, and made us take off our comfortable robes of peace so that we could crush our old limbs in ungentle steel armor. This is not as it should be, my lord. What do you say now? Will you untie this ill-tempered knot of hateful war? Will you move again in that obedient orbit where you did give a fair and natural light, and will you cease to be a comet going its own way and showing itself to be a terrifying omen and a sign of evil soon to come? A dutiful subject should revolve around his King in an obedient orbit, but you do not do so."

"Hear me, my liege," Worcester said. "For my own part, I could be well content to spend the end of my life in peaceful and quiet hours. I have not sought this day of battle."

"You have not sought it!" the King said. "How has it come, then?"

Falstaff said, "Rebellion lay in his way, and he found it."

Prince Hal said to Falstaff, "Shut up, you chattering fool."

Worcester said to the King, "It pleased your majesty to turn your looks of favor away from myself and all the Percys, and yet I must remind you, my lord, we were the first and dearest of your friends. For you I broke my staff of office under King Richard II, and I rode swiftly day and night to meet you on the way and kiss your hand, while still you were in position and in reputation not as strong and fortunate as I. It was myself, my brother, and his son who brought you home to England and boldly did face the dangers of the time. You swore to us at Doncaster that you did not intend to challenge the King and that you wanted nothing more than what you had inherited: the Dukedom of Lancaster. We swore that we would help you gain your inheritance.

"But within a short time, good fortune poured on you, and you became ambitious. You had the help of the Percys, and you had the good fortune that King Richard II was absent from England and in Ireland. England was suffering from the abuses of the King, you seemed to have been grievously wronged, and contrary winds kept King Richard II so long in Ireland that everyone in England thought that he was dead.

"You took advantage of these things, and you decided to seize power in your hands. You forgot the oath you made to us at Doncaster. You took advantage of our aid the way that a cuckoo takes advantage of a sparrow. The cuckoo lays its eggs in the nest of a sparrow, and its offspring grows larger than the sparrow's nestlings and pushes them out of the nest. You grew large and powerful because of our feeding you, and you began to oppress us. You had grown so large and powerful that we, your supporters, dared not go near you because of fear that you would swallow us. We were forced, for the sake of safety, to fly with nimble wing out of your sight and raise this army. We have been forced to do this because of things that you have done. You have treated us badly and unnaturally, you have threatened us, and you have violated all the promises you made to us before you became King."

"These things you have indeed articulated," King Henry IV said. "You have proclaimed them in the centers of marketplaces and had them read in churches to adorn the garment of rebellion with some fine color that might please the eyes of fickle turncoats and poor malcontents who stare with their mouths open and then hug themselves with delight at the news of tumultuous rebellion. You are putting lipstick on a pig. Rebels have always come up with weak justifications for bloody warfare; they have never lacked for supporters such as angry beggars who are hungry for pellmell havoc and confusion."

Prince Hal said, "In both armies are many souls who shall pay very dearly with their lives or with grievous injuries if the armies join in battle. Tell your nephew, Hotspur, that the Prince of Wales joins with the entire world to praise him. Except for this rebellion, I swear, I do not think that a nobler gentleman, more active-valiant or more valiant-young, more daring or bolder, than he is now alive to grace this age with noble deeds. For my part — I speak it to my shame — I have neglected my responsibilities. I hear that Hotspur would agree that this is true. Yet let me say this in front of my father: I am willing, although Hotspur has a much better reputation in warfare than do I, to fight him in single combat to the death. Whoever wins the single combat wins the war. I am willing to fight him in order to save bloodshed and lives in both armies."

King Henry IV, who believed that the odds would be against his son, said, "And, Prince of Wales, we would be willing for you to fight Hotspur in single combat, except that infinite reasons are against it. No, Worcester, no, a single combat will not happen."

He added, "We love our people well. We even love those who are misled and are on the side of Hotspur. If they are willing to accept our pardon, then Hotspur and they and you shall be my friends again and I shall be their friend. Tell Hotspur about the pardon I am offering and bring me word of what he will do. Understand that if he will not stop this rebellion and will not accept the pardon, then I will command rebuke and dreadful punishment to go to him and mete out justice. Go now. We need no longer talk. My offer of pardon to you rebels is fair; I advise you to accept it."

Worcester and Sir Richard Vernon left the King's camp.

Prince Hal said, "Your offer of pardon will not be accepted, I swear. Douglas and Hotspur are both confident that they will be victorious in battle."

"Therefore," King Henry IV said, "everyone get ready to attack. Once they answer and decline our pardon, we will set on them and start the battle. May God support us because our cause is just!"

Everyone departed except Prince Hal and Falstaff.

Falstaff said, "Hal, if you see me wounded and down in the battle, bestride me and protect me and save my life. It is what a friend would do."

"Anyone who bestrides your vast bulk would have to be a colossus," Prince Hal replied, "so say your prayers. I need to go now."

"I wish it were bedtime, Hal, and all were well," Falstaff said.

"Why, you owe God your life, and so you owe God a debt," Prince Hal said. "The only way to pay God the debt you owe is with your death."

Prince Hal left to go to his troops and make sure that they were ready for him to lead them into battle.

Falstaff said, "I may owe God a debt, but the debt is not yet due, and I would hate to pay that debt before it is due. God has not appeared before me and demanded that the debt be paid, and I will not go to Him and voluntarily pay the debt. It doesn't matter. Honor spurs me on to go into battle. Yes, but suppose that honor leads me to be killed or wounded in battle? What then? Can honor set a broken leg? No. Can honor set a broken arm? No. Can honor take away the pain of a wound? No. Does honor have skill in surgery, then? No, it does not. What is honor? It is a word. What is in that word 'honor' — what is that honor? It is nothing but the air that we breathe out when we pronounce a word. Who has honor? He who died on Wednesday. Does he feel honor? No. Does he hear it? No. Can it be sensed? Not by the dead. Dead people can have honor, but it is worthless to them. Will honor stay with the living? No. Why not? While people are living, they have detractors — people slander them. Therefore, I'll have nothing to do with honor. Honor is only a coat of arms that identifies a dead nobleman. I now end my catechism."

Many people, if they had witnessed this scene, would think, *A catechism is a series of questions designed to elicit a person's view — for example, about religious matters. Falstaff's religion is to look out for himself. Falstaff regards himself as the most important thing that exists — he regards himself as the center of the universe. Other people often regard something or someone or Someone as being more important than themselves. Those people are not Falstaff.*

Some people, if they had witnessed this scene, would think, *Falstaff is right, you know. It is better to be a live coward than a dead hero.*

Other people, such as Hotspur and Prince Hal, regard honor as worthwhile and important.

In the rebel camp, Worcester said to Sir Richard Vernon, "My nephew Hotspur must not know, Sir Richard, the liberal and kind offer of the King."

"It were best that he did know," Sir Richard Vernon replied.

"If he finds out and accepts the offer, then we are ruined," Worcester said. "I do not believe that it is likely — or even possible — that the King should keep his word and regard us as his friends. He will continue to suspect us of treason and find a time to punish this rebellion at another time and by using some pretext. All our lives he will look at us with suspicion. We raised an army and marched in rebellion against the King. We shall be trusted only as a fox is trusted. A fox may be partially tamed, may be loved, and may be locked up in a cage, but still the fox will retain some of its wildness. No matter how we look, whether we appear to be sad or merry, the King will misinterpret our looks. We shall feed like oxen at a stall; we shall be fattened before we are butchered. My nephew's trespass may be forgotten; Hotspur has the excuse of youth and heat of blood, and with a nickname like Hotspur he may be forgiven on the basis that such a nickname denotes the brain of a hare and a lack of self-control. This rebellion will not lie on Hotspur's head; it will lie on my head and on the head of Hotspur's father. We are the ones who encouraged Hotspur to rebel; he caught his guilt from us like a disease. We, as the genesis of the rebellion, shall pay for it. Therefore, good kinsman, do not let Hotspur know the liberal and kind offer of the King."

Sir Richard Vernon replied, "Say whatever you want to say. I will back you up and say that you are telling the truth. Look, here is Hotspur now."

Hotspur and Douglas met Worcester and Sir Richard Vernon.

Hotspur ordered, "Prepare to release the Lord of Westmoreland. My uncle has returned from seeing the King, and Westmoreland was the hostage who ensured a safe return for my uncle."

He then said to Worcester, "Uncle, what news do you bring from King Henry IV?"

"The King wishes to go into battle quickly."

Douglas said, "Give the Lord of Westmoreland a defiant message to give to the King."

Hotspur replied, "Lord Douglas, go to the Lord of Westmoreland and give him a defiant message to deliver."

"Indeed, I will, and very willingly," Douglas said.

He left to see the Earl of Westmoreland.

"The King will not show us any mercy," Worcester said.

"Did you beg for mercy?" Hotspur asked. "God forbid that you would!"

"I told him gently about our grievances and about his oath-breaking. He replied by lying that he never lied. He called us rebels and traitors, and he said that he will punish our rebellion with his proud and mighty army."

The Earl of Douglas returned from talking with the Earl of Westmoreland.

"Arm yourselves, gentlemen," Douglas said, "and prepare to fight. I have thrown a brave defiance in King Henry IV's teeth. Westmoreland will deliver the message, and as soon as the King hears it, the battle will start."

Worcester said to Hotspur, "The Prince of Wales stepped forth before his father the King, and he challenged you to a single fight."

"I wish that a single fight would decide the victor, and that no one except Prince Hal and I would fight and get out of breath. But tell me what tone he used in his challenge to me. Did he show contempt for me?"

Sir Richard Vernon said, "No, by my soul, he showed no contempt at all for you. I never in my life did hear a challenge urged more modestly, unless a brother should ask his brother to compete in gentle exercise and proof of arms. He gave you all the respect that is due to a man, he praised you with a Princely tongue, he listed your notable qualities in detail like the writer of a history, and he said that praise by itself was not enough to state your true worth. In addition, he did something that showed that he is indeed a Prince: He admitted his faults and regretted his truant youth with such a grace as if he were a teacher teaching a lesson and a student learning one at the same time. He stopped speaking then, but I believe, and I would tell everyone in the world, that if he survives this battle, England has never had a sweeter hope, or one so much misunderstood because of his youthful reckless behavior."

Hotspur replied, "Sir Richard, I think that you have fallen in love with Prince Hal's follies. Never have I heard of any Prince who is so wild a libertine. But be he as he will, yet before nightfall I will embrace him with a soldier's arm, and he shall shrink under my soldier's affection."

To everyone, Hotspur said, "Arm yourselves quickly. Fellows, soldiers, friends, think about what we have to do. I do not have the gift of an eloquent tongue, and so you need to motivate yourselves to fight well in battle."

A messenger arrived and told Hotspur, "My lord, here are letters for you."

Hotspur replied, "I do not have time to read them now."

To everyone he said, "Gentlemen, the time of life is short! To spend the shortness of life in a shameful way would make life too long even if it lasted for only an hour. If we survive this battle and continue to live, we will have conquered a King. If we die, we will have a brave death if we can make Princes die with us! We all have good consciences because we bear arms in a fair cause; our motivation for bearing arms is just."

Another messenger arrived and said, "My lord, prepare to fight. The King is starting to attack."

"I thank the King because he has stopped my speech," Hotspur said. "I prefer not to talk, and I say only this: Let each man do his best. Now I draw my sword, which I intend to stain with the best blood that I can meet in the battle we fight this perilous day. *Esperance*! Hope! Let's go to battle. Sound all the lofty instruments of war, and let us all embrace. By Heaven, we know that some of us never again shall live to embrace friends again!"

They embraced and went off to fight in war.

— 5.3 —

The battle had started. In the battlefield between the two camps, Douglas encountered Sir Walter Blunt, who was dressed like King Henry IV and acting as a decoy.

Sir Walter Blunt asked, "What is your name, you who in the battle thus accosts me? What honor do you think you'll gain by fighting me?"

"My name is Douglas, and I have been seeking you out in this battle because some people tell me that you are King Henry IV."

"They have told you the truth," Sir Walter Blunt lied.

"The Lord of Stafford has paid dearly today for assuming your likeness because of instead of ending your life, King Henry IV, my sword ended his life. My sword will also end your life, King, unless you surrender to me."

"I was not born a quitter, proud Scot. I will not surrender; instead, you shall find in me a King who will get revenge for the death of Lord Stafford."

They fought, and Douglas killed Sir Walter Blunt.

Hotspur ran up to Douglas and said, "If you had fought at Holmedon the way that you are fighting now, you and your Scottish army would have won the battle."

"The battle we are fighting now is over, and we are victorious," Douglas said. "Look! I have killed the King."

"Where is he?" Hotspur asked.

"Here," Douglas said, pointing at the corpse at his feet.

"No, Douglas," Hotspur said. "I know this man's face well. A gallant knight he was, and his name was Sir Walter Blunt. He is dressed as if he were the King."

Douglas said to the corpse, "Wherever your soul goes, let it take with it the title of Fool. You borrowed the title of King, and it has cost you dearly. Why did you tell me that you were King Henry IV?"

"The King has many decoys," Hotspur said. "Many of his noblemen are dressed like him and wearing his coats — vests embroidered with a coat of arms and worn over armor."

"Then I will use my sword to kill all his coats," Douglas said. "I will murder all his wardrobe, piece by piece, until I meet the real King."

"Let's return to the fighting!" Hotspur said. "The battle is going well for us."

They left.

Falstaff walked onto the scene and stood near Sir Walter Blunt's corpse.

He said, "In London, I could often escape paying what I owe by skipping out on the bill, but I am afraid that today I may have to pay the debt I owe to God, and that is a payment in full in which I lose my life."

He noticed the corpse lying nearby: "But who is lying dead here? Sir Walter Blunt. Here is honor! This demonstrates what I said earlier about honor."

He paused, and then he said, "I am as hot as molten lead, and as heavy as it, too. May God keep lead out of me! I need no more weight than my own intestines."

He laughed at his own joke, and then he added, "I have led my company of ragamuffins to where they have been peppered with lead bullets. Not three of my hundred and fifty are left alive; and they are mutilated and will spend the rest of their lives at city gates with other beggars to seek alms."

Falstaff heard a noise and said, "Who's there?"

It was Prince Hal, who had been fighting hard and who had lost his sword in the confusion of battle. This was the day that he had promised himself and his father the King that he would redeem himself, and he was determined to do exactly that.

"Why are you standing here and doing nothing?" Prince Hal said when he saw Falstaff. "Lend me your sword. Many a nobleman lies stark and stiff and dead under the hoofs of horses that bear our boasting enemies. The lives of these dead patriots are not yet avenged. I beg you to lend me your sword."

Falstaff lied, "Hal, please let me rest awhile and get back my breath. Not even Gregory XIII, that Pope and tyrant who encouraged the killing of many French Protestants in the Massacre of Saint Bartholomew's Day, ever did such deeds in arms as I have done this day. I have killed Hotspur; I am sure of that."

"I am just as sure that he is still alive and wants to kill you," Prince Hal said. "Please, lend me your sword."

"No," Falstaff said. "If Hotspur is still alive, then I need my sword to defend myself. But you can have my pistol if you want it."

"Give it to me," Prince Hal said. "What! Is it still in your holster?"

"It is hot, Hal," Falstaff said. "I have fired it so often that it became so hot that I had to put it back in its holster."

He added, "Look in my holster and you will find something that will sack a city."

Prince Hal looked and found a bottle of sack. He pulled it out and said, "Is this a time for jokes?" Then he threw the bottle of sack at Falstaff and ran off to find a weapon and start fighting again.

Falstaff said, "Well, if Hotspur Percy is still alive, I'll pierce him. If he comes across me, so be it, but if he doesn't, I have no intention of going out of my way to get in his way. If I were to be so stupid as to willingly seek him out, I would deserve for him to slice me up the way a butcher does a piece of meat to get it ready for broiling. I like not such grinning honor as the late Sir Walter Blunt has. I prefer life. If I can save my life, well and good. If I cannot save my life, then unlooked-for honor comes to me and that is the end of me."

— 5.4 —

In another part of the battlefield a little later were Prince Hal, who was bleeding, King Henry IV, Lord John of Lancaster, and the Earl of Westmoreland.

King Henry IV said to Prince Hal, "Please, Harry, withdraw from the battle. You are bleeding too much to continue fighting. Lord John of Lancaster, go with him."

"No, my lord," John of Lancaster said. "I would not leave the battlefield unless I myself were bleeding."

Prince Hal said to his father the King, "I beg your majesty, advance. If you retreat, you will dismay your troops."

"I will do so," the King said. "My Lord of Westmoreland, lead the Prince of Wales to his tent."

"Come, my lord, I'll lead you to your tent," Westmoreland said.

Prince Hal objected, "Lead me, my lord? I do not need your help. God forbid that a shallow scratch should drive the Prince of Wales away from such a battlefield as this, where our noble troops are stained with battle and trodden on by soldiers and horses, and the rebels triumph with their massacres!"

"We have rested too long," Lord John of Lancaster said. "Come, Westmoreland, our duty lies this way. Let us do our duty."

Lord John of Lancaster and the Earl of Westmoreland left to rejoin the battle.

Prince Hal said about Lord John, his younger brother, "By God, you have deceived me, Lancaster. I did not think that you had such a brave spirit. Before, I loved you as a brother, John; but now, I respect you as I respect my soul."

King Henry IV said, "I saw John fight Hotspur with his sword. John fought harder and better than I expected such a young warrior to fight."

"This boy gives courage to us all!" Prince Hal said.

Then he left to rejoin the battle.

Douglas appeared, saw King Henry IV, and said, "Another King! They grow like Hydra's heads. Each time Hercules fought the mythological creature and cut off one of its heads, two more grew in its place. I am Douglas, fatal to all those who wear those colors on their vests. Who are you, you counterfeiter of the person of the King?"

"I am the King himself, and Douglas, I grieve because you have killed so many of the brave men who are pretending to be me. It would have been much better if you had found me. Two of my sons are seeking Hotspur and you on the battlefield, but since you and I have met, I will fight you, so defend yourself."

"I fear that you are another counterfeit," Douglas said, "but yet you bear yourself like a King. Whoever you are, I will fight you and I will kill you."

They fought, and Douglas fought better. The King was in danger of being killed when Prince Hal saw the fight and came running to save his father's life.

"Surrender, vile Scot," Prince Hal said, "or you will never hold up your head again. The spirits of valiant Stafford, Shirley, and Blunt, all of whom have died on this battlefield, are in my arms. It is the Prince of Wales who threatens you, and I never promise anything but what I intend to do."

The fought, and Douglas ended up fleeing from Prince Hal, who saved his father's life.

Prince Hal said to his father, "Be happy, my lord. How are you? Sir Nicholas Gawsey has sent to ask for help. So has Clifton. I am going to Clifton now."

"Stay, and rest awhile," the King said. "You have redeemed your bad reputation, and you have shown that you put some value on my life by rescuing me like this."

"People have done me a great injury by saying that I want you to die," Prince Hal said. "If that were true, I would have let Douglas kill you, which he would have done as quickly as all the poisons in the world, thus saving any treacherous labor by me, your son."

"You go and help Clifton," the King said. "I will go and help Sir Nicholas Gawsey."

King Henry IV departed.

Hotspur came onto the scene and saw Prince Hal.

Hotspur said, "Unless I am mistaken, you are the Prince of Wales."

"You speak as if I would deny who I am," Prince Hal replied.

"My name is Harry Percy. People call me Hotspur."

"Why, then I see a very valiant rebel," Prince Hal said. "I truly am the Prince of Wales. Hotspur, do not think to share glory with me anymore. Two planets do not share one orbit, and England cannot endure a double reign of Hotspur and the Prince of Wales."

"Nor shall it, Prince Hal," Hotspur replied. "The hour has come in which one of us will die. I wish to God that your reputation in battle were as great as is my reputation."

"I will make my reputation better than it is before I part from you," Prince Hal said. "All of the honors that you have gathered I will reap and use to make a garland for my head."

"I can no longer tolerate your empty boasts," Hotspur said.

Hotspur and Prince Hal fought.

Falstaff arrived and cheered on Prince Hal: "Well done, Hal. Go to it. You shall find no boy's play here, I tell you."

Douglas happened onto the scene, and he began to fight Falstaff, who pretended to have a heart attack and fell down "dead."

Douglas, who did not recognize the Prince of Wales and who thought that Hotspur was a better warrior than the man he was currently fighting, left, and Prince Hal and Hotspur continued to fight.

Prince Hal dealt Hotspur a mortal blow with his sword, and Hotspur fell and said, "Prince of Wales, you have robbed me of my youth! I better endure the loss of brittle life than I endure the loss of my proud titles that you have taken from me. Their loss wounds my thoughts worse than your sword wounds my flesh. Our thoughts are dependent on our bodies, and our bodies are dependent on time. And time, which sees all of existence, must come to an end. As a dying man, I can prophesy, but the earthly and cold hand of death lies on my tongue. Hotspur, you have no time to prophesy because you are dust and food for —"

Hotspur died.

Prince Hal finished Hotspur's last sentence: "For worms, brave Hotspur. Fare thee well, great heart! Misguided ambition, how much have you shrunk! When this body contained a spirit, a kingdom was too small a territory for it, but now two paces of the vilest earth is room enough to make a grave to contain it. This earth on which you lie dead will never bear a living man as valiant as you. If you were capable of hearing me, I would not give you so much praise, but now that you are dead, let me cover your mangled face. On your behalf, I will thank myself for performing this rite of tender duty to the dead. Goodbye, and take my praise of you with you to Heaven! Let your rebellion sleep with you in your grave and not be mentioned in your epitaph."

Prince Hal saw Falstaff lying "dead" on the ground.

"What, old acquaintance! Could not all this flesh keep in a little life? Poor Jack, farewell! I could have better spared a better man. I should heavily — in more ways than one — miss you, if I were much in love with frivolity! Death has not struck so fat a deer today, although it has struck many dearer, in this bloody fray. I will see to it that you are quickly disemboweled for embalming. Until then, lie here dead in the blood of this battlefield."

Prince Hal left.

Falstaff got up off the ground and said, "Disemboweled! If you disembowel me today, I give you permission to salt me and eat me tomorrow. By God, it was time for me to counterfeit death, or that raging and bloodthirsty Scot had taken my life! But is 'counterfeit' the right word? I am no counterfeit. A counterfeit of a man does not have the life of a man. To do as I did — to counterfeit dying so that I could continue living — is to be no counterfeit, but instead to be the true and perfect image of life. The better part of valor is discretion; that is, the most important part of courage is caution. By being cautious and counterfeiting death rather than fighting, I have saved my life."

Falstaff looked at Hotspur's corpse and said, "By God, I am afraid of this volatile and easily inflamed Hotspur, although he is dead. What if he is also counterfeiting death and will soon get up? I am afraid that he will prove to be a better actor than I am. Therefore, I will make sure that he is dead, and I will swear that I killed him. Why may not he rise as well as I did? Only a witness could prove that to be wrong, and the only witnesses are my own eyes — nobody sees me."

Falstaff stabbed Hotspur's corpse and said, "You now have a new wound in your thigh, and I will take you along with me."

Falstaff picked up Hotspur's corpse in preparation of carrying it to someone in authority so that he could get a reward.

Prince Hal and Lord John of Lancaster arrived on the scene.

Prince Hal said, "Brother John, today you have very bravely fought in your first battle and bloodied your sword."

John of Lancaster saw Falstaff and said, "Who is this? Didn't you tell me that this fat man was dead?"

"I did say that," Prince Hal said. "I saw him dead; he was lying breathless and bleeding on the ground."

Prince Hal said to Falstaff, "Are you alive? Are my eyes imagining things? Please, speak. I will not trust my eyes until I have the evidence of my ears to support them. You cannot be what you seem to be!"

"I am not a ghost — that's for sure," Falstaff replied. "But if I am not Jack Falstaff, then I am a rascal."

Falstaff dropped on the ground the corpse he was carrying and said, "There is Hotspur. If your father the King will reward me, well and good. If he will not, then let him kill the next Hotspur himself. I look to be made either an Earl or a Duke, I can assure you."

"Why, I killed Hotspur myself and I saw you lying dead," Prince Hal said.

"Did you?" Falstaff said. "Really? How this world is given to lying! I grant you that I was down and out of breath, and so was Hotspur, but we both rose simultaneously and fought a long hour by Shrewsbury clock. If I may be believed, well and good; if not, let them who should reward courage bear the sin upon their own heads. I swear by my eternal soul that I gave Hotspur this wound in the thigh. If any man alive denies it, I will make him eat a piece of my sword."

Lord John said, "This is the strangest tale that I ever heard."

"And this is the strangest fellow, brother John," Prince Hal said.

He said to Falstaff, "Come, bring your luggage — Hotspur's corpse — nobly on your back. For my part, if this lie of yours will do you any good, I will not openly contradict you but will let you get away with it."

They heard a military trumpet.

Prince Hal said, "The trumpet sounds retreat for the rebels; the day is ours. We have won the battle. Come, brother, let us go to the highest ground on the battlefield to see which of our friends are living, and which are dead."

Prince Hal and John of Lancaster left, leaving Falstaff alone with Hotspur's corpse.

"I will follow them so that I can collect a reward," Falstaff said. "May God reward whoever rewards me! If I am rewarded with a title of greatness such as Earl or Duke, I will grow less because I will repent, go on a diet, stop drinking sack, and live as cleanly as a nobleman should."

King Henry IV, in the presence of Prince Hal, Lord John of Lancaster, and the Earl of Westmoreland, was ready to pass judgment on the captured Earl of Worcester and Sir Richard Vernon.

He said, "Rebellion always ends in shame and disgrace and defeat. Ill-spirited Worcester! Did not we send assurances of mercy, pardon, and expressions of friendship to all of you? And yet you said that I did the opposite! Hotspur trusted you, and you lied to him! Three knights who fought for me are dead today, and so are an Earl and many more people who would still be alive if you had acted like a Christian and had reported truthfully my offer of friendship and pardon."

Worcester replied, "What I have done I did out of regard for my safety. I await my fate patiently and calmly because I have no way to avoid it."

"Execute Worcester and Sir Richard Vernon," King Henry IV ordered. "I will think about which punishments to give to other rebels."

Guards took Worcester and Sir Richard Vernon away.

King Henry IV asked, "What is happening on the battlefield?"

Prince Hal said, "The noble Scot, Lord Douglas, when he saw that the rebels had lost the battle, that Hotspur had been killed, and that all his soldiers were fleeing in terror, fled with his soldiers. He fell from a crag and hit the ground so hard that he was stunned and then captured. Douglas is in my tent under guard. I ask your grace for permission to decide what to do with him."

"I grant you that permission with all my heart," King Henry IV said. This was a way to reward Prince Hal for saving his life and for the Prince's courage in the battle.

Prince Hal said, "Then, brother John of Lancaster, to you I give the honor of doing this act: Go to Douglas and release him to freely go wherever he will, without having to pay a ransom. The courage he showed in battle against us today has taught us how to cherish such high deeds even though he was our enemy." Prince Hal, like Worcester and Hotspur before him, knew that this was a way to turn an enemy into a friend. He also knew that this was a way to reward his brother John for his courage in the battle.

John of Lancaster said, "I thank your grace for this gracious assignment, and I shall inform Douglas immediately that he is free."

King Henry IV knew that the battle was won, but that the war continued.

He said, "We have more battles to fight. We will divide our army in two. You, son John, and my kinsman Westmoreland shall take half the army and go towards York as quickly as you can to fight Northumberland and the Archbishop of York — the prelate Scroop — who, I have been informed, are busily raising an army to fight us. I and you, son Harry, will take the other half of the army and go to Wales to fight the army of Glendower and his son-in-law Mortimer, the Earl of March."

He added, "Rebellion in this land shall lose its sway, when it meets the check of another battle on another day. Our work today has been so well done that we will not quit until this war we have won."

APPENDIX A: BRIEF HISTORICAL BACKGROUND

KING RICHARD I: 1189-1199

He was also known as Richard the Lionheart because of his military prowess as a leader and soldier. He was a Christian commander in the Third Crusade. As King, he spent little time in England. Much of his time was spent defending his lands in France. He also spent time in captivity.

KING JOHN: 1199-1216

He was also known as John Lackland because he lost the Duchy of Normandy and most of his lands in France. In 1215, he signed the Magna Carta. King John is a bad King in Robin Hood stories.

KING HENRY III: 1216-1272

Son of King John, he reigned for 56 years. At the beginning of his reign, much of England was controlled by the French Prince Louis (later King Louis VIII), but at the end of his reign, England was controlled by the King of England.

KING EDWARD I: 1272-1307

Edward Longshanks fought and defeated the Welsh chieftains, and he made his eldest son the Prince of Wales. He won victories against the Scots, and he brought the coronation stone from Scone to Westminster.

KING EDWARD II: 1307-deposed 1327

At the Battle of Bannockburn in 1314, the Scots defeated his army. His wife and her lover, Mortimer, deposed him. According to legend, he was murdered in Berkeley Castle by means of a red-hot poker thrust up his anus.

KING EDWARD III: 1327-1377

Son of King Edward II, he reigned for a long time — 50 years. Because he wanted to conquer Scotland and France, he started the Hundred Years War in 1338. King Edward III and his eldest son, Edward the Black Prince, won important victories against the French in the Battle of Crécy (1346) and the Battle of Poitiers (1356).

One of King Edward III's sons was John of Gaunt, first Duke of Lancaster.

Another of King Edward III's sons was Edmund of Langley, first Duke of York.

During his reign, the Black Death — the bubonic plague — struck in 1348-1350 and killed half of England's population.

KING RICHARD II: 1377-deposed 1399

King Richard II was the son of Edward the Black Prince. In 1381, Wat Tyler led the Peasants Revolt, which was suppressed. King Richard II sent Henry, Duke of Lancaster, into exile and seized Henry's estates, but in 1399 Henry, Duke of Lancaster, returned from exile and deposed King Richard II, thereby becoming King Henry IV. In 1400, King Richard II was murdered in Pontefract Castle, which is also known as Pomfret Castle.

HOUSE OF LANCASTER

KING HENRY IV: 1399-1413

Henry, Duke of Lancaster, was the son of John of Gaunt, who was the third son of King Edward III. He was born at Bolingbroke Castle and so was also known as Henry of Bolingbroke. Returning from exile in France to reclaim his estates, he deposed King Richard II. He spent the 13 years of his reign putting down rebellions and defending himself against those who would assassinate or depose him. The Welshman Owen Glendower and the English Percy family were among those who fought against him. King Henry IV died at the age of 45.

KING HENRY V: 1413-1422

The son of King Henry IV, he was known as Prince Hal before becoming King. King Henry V renewed the war with France. He and his army defeated the French at the Battle of Agincourt (1415) despite being heavily outnumbered. He married Catherine of Valoise, the daughter of the French King, but he died before becoming King of France. He left behind a 10-month-old son, who became King Henry VI.

KING HENRY VI: 1422-deposed 1461; briefly returned to the throne in 1470-1471

The Hundred Years War ended in 1453; the English lost all land in France except for Calais, a port city. After King Henry VI suffered an attack of mental illness in 1454, Richard, third Duke of York and the father of King Henry IV and King Richard III, was made Protector of the Realm. England suffered civil war after the House of York challenged King Henry VI's right to be King of England. In 1470, King Henry VI was briefly restored to the English throne. In 1471, he was murdered in the Tower of London. A short time previously, his son, Edward, Prince of Wales, had been killed at the Battle of Tewkesbury in 1471; this was the final battle in the Wars of the Roses. The Yorkists decisively defeated the Lancastrians.

King Henry VI founded both Eton College and King's College, Cambridge.

WARS OF THE ROSES

From 1455-1487, the Yorkists and the Lancastrians fought for power in England in the famous Wars of the Roses. The emblem of the York family was a white rose, and the emblem of the Lancaster family was a red rose. The Yorkists and the Lancastrians were descended from King Edward III.

HOUSE OF YORK

KING EDWARD IV: 1461-1483 (King Henry VI briefly returned to the throne in 1470-1471)

Son of Richard, third Duke of York, he charged his brother George, Duke of Clarence, with treason and had him murdered in 1478. After dying suddenly, he left behind two sons aged 12 and 9, and five daughters.

His surviving two brothers in Shakespeare's play *Richard III* are these: 1) George, Duke of Clarence. Clarence is the second-oldest brother; and 2) Richard, Duke of Gloucester, and afterwards King Richard III. Gloucester is the youngest surviving brother.

William Caxton established the first printing press in Westminster during King Edward IV's reign.

KING EDWARD V: 1483-1483

The eldest son of King Edward IV, he reigned for only two months, the shortest-lived monarch in English history. He was 13 years old. He and his younger brother, Richard, were murdered in the Tower of London. According to Shakespeare's play, their uncle, Richard, Duke of Gloucester, who became King Richard III, was responsible for their murders.

KING RICHARD III: 1483-1485

Brother of King Edward IV, Richard, the Duke of Gloucester, declared the two Princes in the Tower of London — King Edward V and Richard, Duke of York — illegitimate and made himself King Richard III. In 1485, Henry Tudor, Earl of Richmond, a descendant of John of Gaunt, who was the father of King Henry IV, defeated King Richard III at the Battle of Bosworth Field in Leicestershire. King Richard III died in that battle.

King Richard III's father was Richard Plantagenet, Duke of York. His mother was Cecily Neville, Duchess of York.

King Richard III's death in the Battle of Bosworth Field is regarded as marking the end of the Middle Ages in England.

A NOTE ON THE PLANTAGENETS

The first Plantagenet King was King Henry II (1154-1189). From 1154 until 1485, when King Richard III died, all English kings were Plantagenets. Both the Lancaster family and the York family were Plantagenets.

Geoffrey Plantagenet, Count of Anjou, was the founder of the House of Plantagenet. Geoffrey's son, Henry Curtmantle, became King Henry II of England, thereby founding the Plantagenet dynasty. Geoffrey wore a sprig of broom, a flowering shrub, as a badge; the Latin name for broom is *planta genista*, and from it the name "Plantagenet" arose.

The Plantagenet dynasty can be divided into three parts:

1154-1216: The Angevins. The Angevin Kings were Henry II, Richard I (Richard the Lionheart), and John 1.

1216-1399: The Plantagenets. These Kings ranged from King Henry III to King Richard II.

1399-1485: The Houses of Lancaster and of York. These Kings ranged from King Henry IV to King Richard III.

BEGINNING OF THE TUDOR DYNASTY

KING HENRY VII: 1485-1509

When King Richard III fell at the Battle of Bosworth, Henry Tudor, Earl of Richmond, became King Henry VII. A Lancastrian, he married Elizabeth of York — young Elizabeth of York in Shakespeare's play *Richard III* — and united the two warring houses, York and Lancaster, thus ending the Wars of the Roses. One of his grandfathers was Sir Owen Tudor, who married Catherine of Valoise, widow of King Henry V.

KING HENRY VIII: 1509-1547

King Henry VIII had six wives. These are their fates: "Divorced, Beheaded, Died, Divorced, Beheaded, Survived." He divorced his first wife, Catherine of Aragon, so that he could marry Anne Boleyn. Because of this, England divorced itself from the Catholic Church, and King Henry VIII became the head of the Church of England. King Henry VIII had one son and two daughters, all of whom became rulers of England: Edward, daughter of Jane Seymour; Mary, daughter of Catherine of Aragon; and Elizabeth, daughter of Anne Boleyn.

KING EDWARD VI: 1547-1553

The son of Henry VIII and Jane Seymour, King Edward VI succeeded his father at the age of nine; a Council of Regency with his uncle, Duke of Somerset, styled Protector, ruled the government.

During King Edward VI's reign, Archbishop Thomas Cranmer wrote the 1549 Book of Common Prayer.

When King Edward VI died, Lady Jane Grey was proclaimed Queen, but she ruled for only nine days before being executed in 1554, aged 17. Mary, daughter of Catherine of Aragon, became Queen. She was Catholic, thus the attempt to make Lady Jane Grey, a Protestant, Queen.

QUEEN MARY I (BLOODY MARY) 1553-1558

Queen Mary I attempted to make England a Catholic nation again. Some Protestant bishops, including Archbishop Thomas Cranmer, were burnt at the stake, and other violence broke out, resulting in her being known as Bloody Mary.

QUEEN ELIZABETH I: 1558-1603

The daughter of King Henry VIII and Anne Boleyn, Queen Elizabeth I was a popular Queen. In 1588, the English navy decisively defeated the Spanish Armada. England had many notable playwrights and poets, including William Shakespeare and Ben Jonson, during her reign. She never married and had no children.

KING JAMES I OF ENGLAND: A MEMBER OF THE HOUSE OF STUART

KING JAMES I OF ENGLAND AND VI OF SCOTLAND: 1603-1625

King James I of England was the son of Mary, Queen of Scots, and Lord Darnley. In 1605 Guy Fawkes and his Catholic co-conspirators were captured before they could blow up the Houses of Parliament; this was known as the Gunpowder Plot.

In 1611, during King James I's reign, the Authorized Version of the Bible (the King James Version) was completed.

Also during King James I's reign, in 1620 the Pilgrims sailed for America in their ship *The Mayflower*.

A NOTE ON SHAKESPEARE

William Shakespeare lived under two monarchs: Queen Elizabeth I and King James I.

APPENDIX B: ABOUT THE AUTHOR

It was a dark and stormy night. Suddenly a cry rang out, and on a hot summer night in 1954, Josephine, wife of Carl Bruce, gave birth to a boy — me. Unfortunately, this young married couple allowed Reuben Saturday, Josephine's brother, to name their first-born. Reuben, aka "The Joker," decided that Bruce was a nice name, so he decided to name me Bruce Bruce. I have gone by my middle name — David — ever since.

Being named Bruce David Bruce hasn't been all bad. Bank tellers remember me very quickly, so I don't often have to show an ID. It can be fun in charades, also. When I was a counselor as a teenager at Camp Echoing Hills in Warsaw, Ohio, a fellow counselor gave the signs for "sounds like" and "two words," then she pointed to a bruise on her leg twice. Bruise Bruise? Oh yeah, Bruce Bruce is the answer!

Uncle Reuben, by the way, gave me a haircut when I was in kindergarten. He cut my hair short and shaved a small bald spot on the back of my head. My mother wouldn't let me go to school until the bald spot grew out again.

Of all my brothers and sisters (six in all), I am the only transplant to Athens, Ohio. I was born in Newark, Ohio, and have lived all around Southeastern Ohio. However, I moved to Athens to go to Ohio University and have never left.

At Ohio U, I never could make up my mind whether to major in English or Philosophy, so I got a bachelor's degree with a double major in both areas, then I added a master's degree in English and a master's degree in Philosophy. Yes, I have my MAMA degree.

Currently, and for a long time to come (I eat fruits and veggies), I am spending my retirement writing books such as *Nadia Comaneci: Perfect 10*, *The Funniest People in Dance*, *Homer's* Iliad: *A Retelling in Prose*, and *William Shakespeare's* Othello: *A Retelling in Prose*.

By the way, my sister Brenda Kennedy writes romances such as *A New Beginning* and *Shattered Dreams*.

APPENDIX C: SOME BOOKS BY DAVID BRUCE

Retellings of a Classic Work of Literature

Arden of Faversham: *A Retelling*

Ben Jonson's The Alchemist: *A Retelling*

Ben Jonson's The Arraignment, or Poetaster: *A Retelling*

Ben Jonson's Bartholomew Fair: *A Retelling*

Ben Jonson's The Case is Altered: *A Retelling*

Ben Jonson's Catiline's Conspiracy: *A Retelling*

Ben Jonson's The Devil is an Ass: *A Retelling*

Ben Jonson's Epicene: *A Retelling*

Ben Jonson's Every Man in His Humor: *A Retelling*

Ben Jonson's Every Man Out of His Humor: *A Retelling*

Ben Jonson's The Fountain of Self-Love, or Cynthia's Revels: *A Retelling*

Ben Jonson's The Magnetic Lady, or Humors Reconciled: *A Retelling*

Ben Jonson's The New Inn, or The Light Heart: *A Retelling*

Ben Jonson's Sejanus' Fall: *A Retelling*

Ben Jonson's The Staple of News: *A Retelling*

Ben Jonson's A Tale of a Tub: *A Retelling*

Ben Jonson's Volpone, or the Fox: *A Retelling*

Christopher Marlowe's Complete Plays: Retellings

Christopher Marlowe's Dido, Queen of Carthage: *A Retelling*

Christopher Marlowe's Doctor Faustus: *Retellings of the 1604 A-Text and of the 1616 B-Text*

Christopher Marlowe's Edward II: *A Retelling*

Christopher Marlowe's The Massacre at Paris: *A Retelling*

Christopher Marlowe's The Rich Jew of Malta: *A Retelling*

Christopher Marlowe's Tamburlaine, Parts 1 and 2: *Retellings*

Dante's Divine Comedy: *A Retelling in Prose*

Dante's Inferno: *A Retelling in Prose*

Dante's Purgatory: *A Retelling in Prose*

Dante's Paradise: *A Retelling in Prose*

The Famous Victories of Henry V: *A Retelling*

From the Iliad *to the* Odyssey: *A Retelling in Prose of Quintus of Smyrna's* Posthomerica

George Chapman, Ben Jonson, and John Marston's Eastward Ho! *A Retelling*

George Peele's The Arraignment of Paris: *A Retelling*

George Peele's The Battle of Alcazar: *A Retelling*

George Peele's David and Bathsheba, and the Tragedy of Absalom: *A Retelling*

George Peele's Edward I: *A Retelling*

George Peele's The Old Wives' Tale: *A Retelling*

George-a-Greene: *A Retelling*

The History of King Leir: *A Retelling*

Homer's Iliad: *A Retelling in Prose*

Homer's Odyssey: *A Retelling in Prose*

J.W. Gent.'s The Valiant Scot: *A Retelling*

Jason and the Argonauts: A Retelling in Prose of Apollonius of Rhodes' Argonautica

John Ford: Eight Plays Translated into Modern English

John Ford's The Broken Heart: *A Retelling*

John Ford's The Fancies, Chaste and Noble: *A Retelling*

John Ford's The Lady's Trial: *A Retelling*

John Ford's The Lover's Melancholy: *A Retelling*

John Ford's Love's Sacrifice: *A Retelling*

John Ford's Perkin Warbeck: *A Retelling*

John Ford's The Queen: *A Retelling*

John Ford's 'Tis Pity She's a Whore: *A Retelling*

John Lyly's Campaspe: *A Retelling*

John Lyly's Endymion, The Man in the Moon: *A Retelling*

John Lyly's Galatea: *A Retelling*

John Lyly's Love's Metamorphosis: *A Retelling*

John Lyly's Midas: *A Retelling*

John Lyly's Mother Bombie: *A Retelling*

John Lyly's Sappho and Phao: *A Retelling*

John Lyly's The Woman in the Moon: *A Retelling*

John Webster's The White Devil: *A Retelling*

King Edward III: *A Retelling*

Mankind: *A Medieval Morality Play* (A Retelling)

Margaret Cavendish's The Unnatural Tragedy: *A Retelling*

The Merry Devil of Edmonton: *A Retelling*

The Summoning of Everyman: *A Medieval Morality Play* (A Retelling)

Robert Greene's Friar Bacon and Friar Bungay: *A Retelling*

The Taming of a Shrew: *A Retelling*

Tarlton's Jests: A Retelling

Thomas Middleton's A Chaste Maid in Cheapside: *A Retelling*

Thomas Middleton's Women Beware Women: *A Retelling*

Thomas Middleton and Thomas Dekker's The Roaring Girl: *A Retelling*

Thomas Middleton and William Rowley's The Changeling: *A Retelling*

The Trojan War and Its Aftermath: Four Ancient Epic Poems

Virgil's Aeneid: *A Retelling in Prose*

William Shakespeare's 5 Late Romances: Retellings in Prose

William Shakespeare's 10 Histories: Retellings in Prose

William Shakespeare's 11 Tragedies: Retellings in Prose

William Shakespeare's 12 Comedies: Retellings in Prose

William Shakespeare's 38 Plays: Retellings in Prose
William Shakespeare's 1 Henry IV, aka Henry IV, Part 1: *A Retelling in Prose*
William Shakespeare's 2 Henry IV, aka Henry IV, Part 2: *A Retelling in Prose*
William Shakespeare's 1 Henry VI, aka Henry VI, Part 1: *A Retelling in Prose*
William Shakespeare's 2 Henry VI, aka Henry VI, Part 2: *A Retelling in Prose*
William Shakespeare's 3 Henry VI, aka Henry VI, Part 3: *A Retelling in Prose*
William Shakespeare's All's Well that Ends Well: *A Retelling in Prose*
William Shakespeare's Antony and Cleopatra: *A Retelling in Prose*
William Shakespeare's As You Like It: *A Retelling in Prose*
William Shakespeare's The Comedy of Errors: *A Retelling in Prose*
William Shakespeare's Coriolanus: *A Retelling in Prose*
William Shakespeare's Cymbeline: *A Retelling in Prose*
William Shakespeare's Hamlet: *A Retelling in Prose*
William Shakespeare's Henry V: *A Retelling in Prose*
William Shakespeare's Henry VIII: *A Retelling in Prose*
William Shakespeare's Julius Caesar: *A Retelling in Prose*
William Shakespeare's King John: *A Retelling in Prose*
William Shakespeare's King Lear: *A Retelling in Prose*
William Shakespeare's Love's Labor's Lost: *A Retelling in Prose*
William Shakespeare's Macbeth: *A Retelling in Prose*
William Shakespeare's Measure for Measure: *A Retelling in Prose*
William Shakespeare's The Merchant of Venice: *A Retelling in Prose*
William Shakespeare's The Merry Wives of Windsor: *A Retelling in Prose*
William Shakespeare's A Midsummer Night's Dream: *A Retelling in Prose*
William Shakespeare's Much Ado About Nothing: *A Retelling in Prose*
William Shakespeare's Othello: *A Retelling in Prose*
William Shakespeare's Pericles, Prince of Tyre: *A Retelling in Prose*
William Shakespeare's Richard II: *A Retelling in Prose*
William Shakespeare's Richard III: *A Retelling in Prose*
William Shakespeare's Romeo and Juliet: *A Retelling in Prose*
William Shakespeare's The Taming of the Shrew: *A Retelling in Prose*
William Shakespeare's The Tempest: *A Retelling in Prose*
William Shakespeare's Timon of Athens: *A Retelling in Prose*
William Shakespeare's Titus Andronicus: *A Retelling in Prose*
William Shakespeare's Troilus and Cressida: *A Retelling in Prose*
William Shakespeare's Twelfth Night: *A Retelling in Prose*
William Shakespeare's The Two Gentlemen of Verona: *A Retelling in Prose*
William Shakespeare's The Two Noble Kinsmen: *A Retelling in Prose*
William Shakespeare's The Winter's Tale: *A Retelling in Prose*

www.ingramcontent.com/pod-product-compliance
Lightning Source LLC
Chambersburg PA
CBHW031337160726
47993CB00002B/717